The
Brides
of
High Hill

The Brides of High Hill

NGHI VO

TOR PUBLISHING GROUP

NEW YORK

THE BRIDES OF HIGH HILL

Copyright © 2024 by Nghi Vo

A Tordotcom Book
Published by Tom Doherty Associates / Tor Publishing Group
120 Broadway
New York, NY 10271

www.torpublishinggroup.com

Tor® is a registered trademark of Macmillan Publishing Group, LLC.

The Library of Congress Cataloging-in-Publication Data is available upon request.

ISBN 978-1-250-85144-4 (hardcover)
ISBN 978-1-250-83803-2 (ebook)

Our books may be purchased in bulk for promotional, educational, or business use. Please contact your local bookseller or the Macmillan Corporate and Premium Sales Department at 1-800-221-7945, extension 5442, or by email at MacmillanSpecialMarkets@macmillan.com.

First Edition: 2024

Printed in the United States of America

0 9 8 7 6 5 4 3 2 1

for Shelby

The
Brides
of
High Hill

Chapter One

Cleric Thien was telling them that it always started with a story.

"What does?" Chih asked. In their dream, they were deeply frustrated and impatient, almost angry. Cleric Thien, as composed in dreams as they had been in life, only continued making their obeisance to Gentleman Bell, kissing his coin and pricking their finger to drip a minuscule amount of blood into the offering bowl.

"Everything," they said without turning around. "The world starts with a story. So do dynasties and eras and wars. So does love, and so does revenge. Everything starts with a story."

"But what does that *mean*?"

On Cleric Thien's shoulder, their neixin and beloved companion, Myriad Virtues, spoke.

"Ask Almost Brilliant," Myriad Virtues advised. "You should ask Almost Brilliant."

The neixin, memory spirits shaped like talking hoopoe birds, remembered every story they had ever been told and every sight they had ever seen. Myriad Virtues was Cleric Thien's neixin just as Almost Brilliant was Chih's, as much a mark of Singing Hills abbey as their indigo robes or their shaved head. Chih touched their shoulder, suddenly more aware of Almost Brilliant's absence than they had been.

"I will, of course I will, but—"

Myriad Virtues was still speaking, or at least, her beak was opening and closing, but Chih couldn't hear her. They tried to get closer, but their limbs were too heavy, and when they tried to move them, they found themself awake.

"Of all the indulgences my precious baby daughter might want, of all the jewels we would buy her and all the books she could read and all the delicious pheasant and rabbit she could eat, she decides that above all things, she must have a cleric!" exclaimed Madame Pham from her corner of the covered ox-cart.

"Ma, please," said Pham Nhung, her voice soft. "We are so far from home, and doesn't their face remind you of Cleric Ly? They look so gentle, and they were so kind to me when I spilled my books all over the road. They helped me pick up every one. I am so grateful they said that they would accompany us to my wedding negotiations to bless me and to keep away the wicked spirits. Can't you be grateful too?"

Chih sat up groggily, trying to rub away the last of their dream. Sleeping this late in the day didn't suit them, and they swallowed a few times to freshen their mouth.

"Of course I will help," they said. "Though I'm sure I told you that Singing Hills has more to do with history than it does with exorcisms."

Madame Pham gave Chih a stern look down her long nose. Like her daughter's, her face was narrow and pale like a grain of rice, but where her daughter had large, wet eyes, hers were squinted with pride and distrust.

"There, you see. We should turn back and get you a better cleric, perhaps someone from the temple of the Lady of a Thousand Hands or the Twins of Jun-li. This one just tells stories."

"I like stories," said Nhung, and she took Chih's hand in hers, smiling shyly.

"That's good, I have a lot," Chih said, momentarily enchanted by Nhung's smile. She smiled close-lipped with one side higher than the other, and it was the prettiest thing Chih had ever seen.

The ox-cart swayed, and Nhung momentarily fell against Chih's side. Her silk robes puffed with the scent of rosewood, and underneath that, Chih, blushing, could smell her skin and her sweat, a little rank after several days' travel. Nhung straightened, pressing her fingers modestly to her cheeks, and Chih sat up straight as well, bearing up under Madame Pham's suspicious eye.

"I tell stories, and I record them as well," Chih said. "That will be a nice thing for your daughter's wedding, won't it, to have it entered into the records at Singing Hills? If Almost Brilliant were here—"

"Such a shame she could not accompany you on this trip," said Nhung. "I wanted very much to meet her. She sounds adorable."

"She might not like to hear you say that," said Chih, "but between the two of us, she really is."

Suddenly Chih missed their companion intensely, and they started to say so, but Master Pham rode up alongside the wagon, pulling even with the rolled-up blind to look in. He was as narrow as his wife and daughter, a little uneasy on his horse, and very stern in the face.

"Are you all well?" he asked, peering in as though he were checking on the state of his hens in the coop. "Little Nhung, have you washed your face and filed your nails for your husband? Are you wearing your best robes?"

"Ba, of course I am ready," Nhung said with what sounded like long patience. "I have waited all my life to become a bride."

Her father looked as if he might have liked to say

more, but his horse snorted, throwing its head back threateningly, and he turned to get it under control as Nhung turned back to Chih.

"My mother has taught me how to run a household, and I believe I am capable, but the reality is so very different, isn't it? I hope I will be a good wife."

"And I hope your husband is worthy of it," Chih said. They had heard many stories throughout their career on the road, and they knew too many where the husbands were nothing of the sort.

"Worthy, unworthy!" cried Madame Pham. "Who gets to speak of worthiness when your father's ship foundered off the coast of the Verdant Islands, when my rotten brother took your grandparents' estate and gambled it away. *Worthy* is *wealthy,* cleric, wealthy enough to keep my precious daughter comfortable all her days."

Chih nodded politely, but they were still grateful to see that Nhung looked faintly rebellious. She didn't look like she would be surprised at the worthiness or lack thereof of her husband, and it would help if she was not startled either way.

The drovers called out, and Nhung sat up straight.

"Doi Cao," she said, her nerves ringing like bells in her voice. "Oh, but it's Doi Cao."

Faster than Chih would have suspected, she pushed open the cart's rear gate, throwing her legs out the door before dropping to the ground.

"Come with me," she implored Chih. "Come with me to see my new home!"

Leaving their bag and studiously avoiding Madame Pham's dire eye, Chih slipped out after her, landing more clumsily than Nhung had from the moving ox-cart. Across the southern part of the empire, ox-carts were the most comfortable and reliable way to travel, but they were exceedingly slow. Nhung and Chih soon outpaced them, coming up on the walls of Doi Cao.

In the capital city of Anh, where the Empress of Wheat and Flood ruled from the mammoth and lion throne, western Ji was considered contested territory, while western Ji considered itself uncontestedly independent. Together, these two things led to a history marked with violence and conflict, evident from the curtain wall around the estate. The wall, as Chih could see when they and Nhung drew near, was a grim and gray thing, likely as thick as a child was tall.

"Oh, but it's ugly," Nhung said with disappointment. "Doi Cao is meant to be so beautiful, a dream from the Ku Dynasty, but look at how ugly this is."

"What a good thing it is that the wall isn't from the Ku Dynasty," said Chih, pleased to be of service. "I've seen walls like that before—they were made to stand up against mammoths during the early reign of the Empress of Salt and Fortune. They were put up hastily, so they are not very attractive, but often they were built to protect things of surpassing loveliness."

Nhung gave Chih a startlingly sly look, that little upturn at the corner of her mouth kicking higher.

"Surpassing loveliness, cleric?"

Chih almost tripped over nothing at all, but then Nhung turned back to the walls, a pensive look on her face.

"If our negotiations go well, this will be my home. I'll live here. Perhaps I will be happy here."

"It is to be most sincerely hoped for, Mistress Nhung," said Chih, who was feeling as if they should be more circumspect.

"Come on. I want to get a little closer. We can double back to the ox-cart so that I may be introduced to my perhaps-husband in a more decorous fashion, but you can only greet your new home once, can't you?"

Up close, the walls of Doi Cao were indeed ugly, mined out of a dark gray stone that had been transported at great cost from foreign quarries. It was heavier and less prone to shattering than the local golden-brown stone, more capable of resisting the concentrated push of an armored mammoth line, and judging from the long, unbroken lines of mortar, this one had.

Against the gray of the wall, Nhung glowed in her peach silk robes, her unbound hair falling past her hips in a black river that devoured the light. As Chih watched, she pressed her cheek against the stone, touching it with almost fearful fingers.

"Hello," she said softly. "Am I home?"

If the stone of Doi Cao answered her, Chih could not hear, and Nhung turned to Chih, taking their hand.

"Thank you for allowing my foolishness. Come on. We should get back before Ma comes after us with the ox-whip."

As they made their way back to the cart, Chih glanced over their shoulder at the wall, gray and silent and scarred. It seemed to them like a poor guarantee for a young woman's happiness, but then what in life gave guarantees?

Chapter Two

The master of Doi Cao had the gates thrown open for the Phams and their retinue, a train of some fifteen carts. It was a fine showing for a wealthy merchant family from the city of Bien Hoa, but Chih noticed as they disembarked how lightly loaded the carts seemed to be, with both people and goods, and they thought of Madame Pham lamenting the family's poor luck at sea and in relatives.

Inside the curtain wall, Doi Cao was every bit the Ku Dynasty dream that Nhung had hoped for, the wide and gracious courtyard clad in pale stone and the broad steps leading up to the entry hall bordered by cedar pillars. The roof was tiled in red ceramic, and running along the topmost ridge and down the angled peaks were the Ku Dynasty's famous slithering beasts.

Noble families invented them in defiance of the

imperial edict that only government buildings could have animal figures on their roofs, and the result was the creation of the crawling figures above, almost animals but not quite, that stared malevolently from the peaks to repel misfortune.

Master Pham handed his daughter down from the ox-cart as if she was too delicate for the very earth, and then with her parents on either side, Nhung approached the stairs where the master of Doi Cao waited.

As they went through the standard formalities, greetings and well-wishes and protestations of humility, Chih took the opportunity to examine Lord Guo. He looked a healthy sixty, likely only a few years off from Nhung's father, but he had a far more powerful build, as broad as both elder Phams put together. Even from where Chih stood with the drovers and the baggage handlers, they could see a raking scar across the side of his face, some old wound grown white and hard. It gave him the look of a soldier turned bureaucrat, and one who had done well for himself given his august surroundings.

It looked as if the greetings were going to go on for a while, so Chih turned to help the baggage handlers unload. It occurred to them that despite the long voyage, their time with the Phams had prevented them from getting to know the handlers at all, which was a shame. The people who worked the artery roads of the empire always had good stories to tell in exchange for some help, but the Phams' hires were cool, turning away pointedly when Chih approached.

In Chih's experience no one wanted to lift a heavy rice chest on their own, but when they persisted, one of the baggage handlers clicked her teeth in frustration and shoved a polished teapot into their hands.

"Here, keep an eye on that, and let us work, honored cleric."

The honorific was second cousin to an actual insult, and Chih backed to the side with a frown, still holding the teapot. They took up a position sheltered by one of the pine trees that grew on either side of the stairs, where the Phams and Lord Guo were still going through the rituals of welcome. The elder Phams offered their best wishes with an eager avidity, Lord Guo accepted them with a comfortable superiority, and Nhung herself stood back with a demure acquiescence that could have been anything from maidenly excitement to stark terror.

"Poor girl."

Chih jumped and turned, startled to see a young man in his sleeping robes in the shadow of the pine. His face was still smooth, but his dark, thick brows and the unhappy set of his jaw made him look older. He was barefoot regardless of the gravel underneath the pine trees, and he watched the party on the stairs with a grim eye.

"Hello," Chih said cautiously. "Why do you say that?"

The young man turned to them. Full on, it was easy to see that he was some relation to Lord Guo, a son or nephew or perhaps even a grandson. Chih expected him to say something about the difference in ages, which was great, or the elder Phams' increasingly obsequious bows.

"Tell her to ask him how many wives he's had."

The young man's face twitched, a pained grimace that had some kind of horrible humor in it.

"They're not in Shu."

He covered his mouth with his hand, and as he walked away, Chih caught a flash of soles that were dark and thick with callouses and a lurch to his stride as if he were going to be sick.

They held the teapot tight to their chest before they remembered and loosed their grip before they could break it. They were just wondering where they could set it down when Nhung appeared.

"Our retainers are going to be stationed outside the walls—my parents rather insisted to make sure Lord Guo didn't see how ragged their uniforms are—but we will be staying in the small hall for guests. Lord Guo asked if we would tour the gardens with him, and my parents are very keen, but I'm afraid that I have a terrible headache."

She offered Chih a hopeful smile, and Chih nodded.

"Is your headache so terrible that perhaps you need to be accompanied to the guest hall?"

"Why, yes, Cleric Chih, thank you for offering!"

Chih smiled, shifting the teapot to one hand and offering Nhung the other. No one really thought of clerics as gallant, least of all themselves, but for Nhung, they could pretend.

The guest hall was an older building, soft but quietly lovely tucked against the lucky east wall. Two ancient purposely dwarfed chestnut trees guarded either side of the stone path, and a slithering beast waited above the covered porch. The tablet by the door designated the house as Eighth Peony.

Nhung's steps slowed and then stopped just short of the hall. She gazed at the house, chewing her lip nervously.

"It looks sort of scary, don't you think?" she asked.

It looked charming and perhaps a little antiquated to Chih, but they only waited as Nhung shifted from foot to foot.

"Perhaps you could go in and look for me?" she asked with a nervous little laugh. It was a laugh that was ready to be laughed at, and Chih squeezed her hand comfortingly.

"All right. Is there anything in particular I should warn you for?"

Nhung's smile became a bit more genuine.

"Will you please look in the rafters and in the corners? When I was young, Ba told me about house sprites, terrible little beings that lurk in the holes of old houses, ready to murder you if you slept where you shouldn't."

"If you don't mind, you should tell me more about them some time, but all right. I'll check."

The steps up to Eighth Peony creaked dramatically under Chih's weight, a design and not an accident, Chih realized with interest. The arrangement of wood would squeak and cry to warn of intruders who didn't know where to step, and they reminded themself to test the steps later so they could write up a complete account for Singing Hills.

Inside, the guest hall had been aired out nicely, screens set up to divide the large open space into a main sitting area with tables, comfortable cushions, and food set out, and smaller spaces set aside for sleeping. There were tapers ready to burn against the night, but with the doors and shutters thrown open, it was still inviting even as the early evening light dimmed to purple.

Dutifully, Chih checked the rafters and the corners as instructed. They did not expect to find anything in such a pleasant space, but Nhung would never trust them again if they were wrong. In the end, the only thing they found was a large hairy spider in a wall niche, and they coaxed it into their hands to bring it outside. As an afterthought, they replaced the spider with the teapot they had been holding. They were somewhat reluctant to let it go—its ceramic weight was comforting in their hands, its roundness fitting their palms perfectly.

"Are you afraid of spiders?" Chih asked. "This one was the only terrible little being I found."

"Oh, I don't care about spiders. But nothing else?"

Chih put the spider down close to the chestnut tree, where it huffily scuttled away.

"No, nothing else. It's as safe as can be. Would you like me to bless it as well?"

Nhung wrinkled her nose at Chih in the most endearing way.

"What good's the blessing of a cleric who sneaks pork whenever no one's looking?"

"Almost as good as that of one who doesn't, I'm told," Chih said, amused. "Come on. There's food inside, and we can find you a place to rest."

They had guessed that Nhung was just seeking a bit of respite from her parents and the pressure of her potential new husband, but as a matter of fact, when they rolled out the thin cotton mattress and shook out the blankets, Nhung crawled right in, turning over five or six times with satisfied groans.

"Braid my hair for me," she demanded sleepily. "Otherwise it will be a rat's nest when I wake up."

"You might say please," Chih said, but they came to sit behind Nhung's back, reaching down to smooth her hair into three even strands. The braid was a clumsy thing—they weren't sure when they had last been called upon to braid anything, let alone the hair of a wealthy girl. Nhung's hair was thick and coarse, and the oil she used left the faintest grease on Chih's fingertips, scenting them with jasmine.

Expensive for her to use so much, Chih thought idly.

Under Chih's touch, Nhung dropped off almost immediately. In sleep, she gained a peace to her features that was mostly absent when she was awake, and by the time Chih finished braiding her hair, she was snoring, a raspy sawing sound that sometimes resolved into a discontented snort.

Adorable, thought Chih, and they went to wash from the basins of water that had been left out and to change into their spare set of robes. They felt refreshed and more alert after, and they remembered that they were quite hungry.

Chih rose and made their way to the front room, where food had been spread out in advance of the Phams' arrival. It was beautiful in the way of cuisine from the capital, a dozen or so small white plates holding single cooked or raw ingredients that could be combined and eaten in a nearly infinite number of combinations.

Lotus nuts and shreds of sweet potato, that's hope for a rich future, dried sardines and fresh shiso leaves, that's luck abroad, I think . . .

Chih sighed, because it would be so easy to steal a scrap or two, but it would also be monstrously impolite, so they slid the door closed behind them and walked out onto the grounds, their small pack with their recording instruments over their shoulder.

The lords and ladies of the Ku Dynasty believed in the harmonious flow of paths through their manors, and as a result, the kitchen was easy to find. It was a building open on one side with a long hearth across the back and a wide table across the front, and it buzzed like a hive of bees with cooks at the fires and a handful of apprentices furiously chopping and prepping at the table.

"Hello," Chih said, sidling up to of the chefs who had stepped out for a breath and to gnaw on a white bun. "I am Cleric Chih. I arrived with the Pham family, and—"

The oldest cook, a short woman with shoulders like boulders, jerked her head in response to Chih's words, not looking away from the shield-sized wok she shook over the fire.

"Five, get them some food and get them out of here."

One of the apprentices stuck his cleaver in his belt and darted into the line with what looked like a fantastic disregard for fire, knives, and verbal abuse. When he emerged, he presented Chih with an earthenware bowl filled with barley porridge and topped with pickled squash, a ladle of pork neck bone broth, and several slices of braised chicken. If he had forgotten that clerics were mostly meant to be vegetarian, Chih was not going to remind him.

"There'll be fancier at the dinner tonight," he said by way of apology, but Chih's stomach was already growling thankfully.

"No, this looks amazing, I can't thank you enough. Can I just pull up a stool here?"

The apprentice's face closed like a door, and Chih wondered if there was something unwilling about it. He looked inclined to be friendly, and closing doors did not seem to come naturally to him.

"Better not," he said. "I don't think it's really. Really proper, you know? You're a cleric with the Pham family, you better go eat at the guest hall or maybe in the gardens. There's herons in the big pond, you could go look at them?"

It was such a transparent evasion that Chih was bemused rather than offended, and they nodded.

"Thank you again for the food. I'll return the bowl when I'm done."

"Oh, just throw it away, don't worry. And we'll bring more food to the guest hall, you don't have to come down here again."

He looked like he wanted to say something else, but the cook shouted him back into line, and never one to push an issue when they had food in hand, Chih took themself off to find a place to eat.

They ended up underneath a willow tree, the withes bending down to touch the grass and the surface of the pond below. The thick green leaves shut out the sound of the manor, and with a breath of relief, Chih sat down to eat. Before they remembered, they plucked some choice bits of chicken out for Almost Brilliant, and then they laughed ruefully at themself. If she were here, she'd laugh at how absent-minded they were when they were distracted.

They were hungrier than they had thought, scraping the bowl with their chopsticks in a way that would have been rude in company and stopping just short of licking out the last bits of sauce.

Finally satisfied, they set the bowl to one side and lay down on the thick grass, using their bag for a pillow. The temperature was dropping in fits and starts, already cooler than it had been when they arrived, and Chih's eyes fluttered closed.

I've been on the road so long. I'm so tired.

Chapter Three

Chih dreamed that the willow withes were really fingers, slender and adorned with rings, and in the pond, there was something with sharp teeth that wanted to suck the willow's flesh from its bones. They were trying to pull the willow's fingers back from the teeth in the water when they were shaken awake with a start.

"Oh, get up, get up, please," Nhung begged.

"I'm up, I'm up!" Chih exclaimed, sitting up.

It was almost full dark, and Nhung's face, painted dead white with two dotted lines of crimson running across her cheeks and another running down her chin, gleamed ghostlike. Her makeup was a work of beauty and skill, but it reduced Nhung's face to the simplest lines, giving her anxiety an almost tangible weight.

"Oh, Chih, the banquet is starting *now,* we have to be there *now,* please!"

Chih started to rise, only to have Nhung lift them

the rest of the way up. Terror gave her wiry frame an unexpected strength, and once she took hold of Chih's arm, she didn't let go, her fingers digging in hard.

"It's all right," Chih said soothingly. "I'm right here, see? I'm not going anywhere."

"He's waiting for me, and my parents couldn't stop talking about what a great man he is, and how much money I could have and how they could finally hold their heads up in public again, and oh, I'm going to cry!"

"Did you know there's a kind of frog in the Arawana steppes that turns into a pebble?"

"What?"

Nhung stared, giving Chih enough time to scoop up their bag and to brush the leaves out of their robes. They had to do this all one-handed, as Nhung did not seem inclined to relinquish their arm.

"It's true. It's a little frog, about the size of a peach pit, and when it gets scared, it goes hard like a rock. Then it flings itself down the slope, bouncing along unhurt as it goes, until it's away from whatever scared it."

"That was a very odd thing to tell me."

"But you're not crying, right?"

Nhung blinked, eyelashes so long they stirred the powder on her face, and she smiled instead.

"No, I'm not. But I'm still terrified."

"That's fine. It would be strange if you weren't. Shall we go to the banquet?"

"Yes, please. Do not leave my side. I am trusting you to protect me if anything awful happens. And if I faint on the doorstep, you have to carry me away, telling everyone that I am too delicate for all of this."

"Be sure I will."

They made their way to the banquet hall, which was lit up with braziers around the perimeter and ornamented with the house guard in splendid blue and gold at every door and window. It was a grand display, wealth and power, but Nhung walked in with her head held high, even if her eyes were demurely cast to the ground.

Before they gained the entrance, Nhung paused on the steps, her gaze coming up at last to look left and right, to breathe and to put a little smile on her face.

"Are you all right?" whispered Chih.

"I believe I will be. There's nothing terrifying in there, is there?"

Some servant must have spied them on the step, because the double doors were thrown open, sparing Chih a response.

"Mistress Pham Nhung, and her companion, Cleric Chih of Singing Hills," announced the steward, and the room rose in respect.

The room had been set up in the style of the capital, with Lord Guo at the head of the hall kneeling at a long low table reserved for his honored guests, and the rest of the party, local nobility and government officials and their wives at a guess, settled at rows of tables facing the front, leaving a long aisle empty in the middle.

There was something too silent and too speculative about the room as they entered, and Nhung shrank a little closer to Chih's side as they passed a delegation from the local temple who gazed at them with censorious frowns.

Lord Guo waited for them at the front of the hall, his face a mask with no telling what lay underneath it.

Nhung dipped in an elegant bow, her hands pressed demurely to her belly, and Chih bowed briefly as well, but no one was looking at them. All eyes were on Nhung, and the moment stretched out as she waited for the lord of the manor to tell her that she might rise.

A moment passed, and then another, and only then did Lord Guo nod with apparent satisfaction.

"Beautiful," he said. "Very beautiful. Come sit by me. Cleric, take your place as well."

Nhung went to sit at Lord Guo's left, and Chih found the cleric's alcove to the lord's right. The cleric's alcove was another fashion from the capital, a sheltered space screened from the rest of the hall, where they could eat their ascetic meals and still whisper counsel to their patrons.

As they settled themself in the cleric's alcove, the noise of the banquet resumed: the elder Phams entering at last with exclamations of praise for the hall and the food, servers rotating with their trays and pouring drinks, people calling to one another from different tables. From their position, Chih had a clear view of Nhung and Lord Guo, her sitting with her head bowed, Lord Guo leaning in to whisper something to her, his hand stroking his beard with contentment.

I suppose it is not a terrible match for the nobility, Chih thought, though they knew very well what they would be saying about it in the kitchen and down in the town. No one liked to see a foal yoked to a worn-out old cart horse, as the saying went, and only a noble family would do something so foolish.

A server came by with a tray for Chih, purple barley, a fan of pickled cucumber, a stack of braised lotus root, and a single puff of golden tofu. It was gorgeously arranged, but Chih was grateful they had eaten before.

At least if anyone peeks in, I won't be gorging myself, they thought with a sigh, picking up the ivory chopsticks.

Beside Lord Guo, Nhung picked at the food on her plate, taking tiny mouthfuls of pork and watercress and lotus by turns. There was something terribly lonely about her, sitting in Lord Guo's shadow, looking out over the assembled party, looking up into the rafters for the monsters of her childhood, only very rarely glancing up at her intended husband, who sat in self-satisfied splendor beside her.

Chih was startled to look over and find Nhung's

eyes on them. When she saw she had Chih's attention, she lifted the cloth napkin to her face as if she was blotting her lips and quickly crossed her eyes and stuck out her tongue, long and red and shocking against the white of her face paint. It was so unexpected that Chih almost choked on their food, and then Nhung set down the napkin, so much the proper prospective bride that it was impossible to imagine her making a face like she just had.

She'll be all right, Chih told themself, and perhaps they would even believe it sooner or later.

The banquet was almost over when there was a commotion at the entrance of the hall. One door rolled open, pushed awkwardly from the outside, and the guard inside the door might have done something about it, but the steward got in his way. The brief confusion allowed a figure in a gleaming white silk wrapper to appear silhouetted by the braziers, his black hair streaming down his shoulders and his eyes black tarns.

He stared around like an animal unused to light before taking a few reeling steps up the center aisle.

"No," he said, the word sloshing around his mouth. "No. No, you *must not*—"

Lord Guo stood from his seat, his face a thundercloud, but Nhung was faster. In a moment, she was down from the dais and approaching the figure at the center of the hall with a sure and certain stride.

"It's all right," she said, her voice soft. "It's all right. No one will."

The young man stared at her, and Chih couldn't say whether it was a sudden clarity in his eyes or another kind of haze dropping over him entirely.

Oh. Oh dear.

Nhung's small hand, her nails painted black and wire-thin gold rings on all her fingers, rose to touch his face gently, tapping with exquisite gentleness over his cheeks, his lips, and his forehead.

"It's all right," she repeated. "It will be all right."

"It won't," the young man said, but he sounded less certain than he had a moment before. "Please. You must not."

Whatever Nhung might have said to that was lost when two men ran through the door, out of breath and fearful.

"Your pardon, lord," one said. "We thought your son was sleeping."

"Did you," said Lord Guo mildly, but a ripple went through the crowd, a tiger only seen in the stirring of the tall grass.

The two men approached Lord Guo's son warily, their hands up to catch or to restrain. Their motions were cautious but practiced, and the one in the rear nodded at Nhung.

"Step back, please, lady," he said, but she ignored

him, still gazing into the eyes of the young man in front of her.

"Lady—"

"I am not a beast," the disheveled man snapped.

He turned, pushing through their hands to stalk to the door. Beyond the hall, a pattering rain cloaked the night, and he and his attendants—jailors, Chih thought uncomfortably—were gone.

Nhung had returned to Lord Guo's side as they all watched the young lord go, so quick that she might never have left her seat at all.

Chih expected some explanation, even if it was only ten or fifteen words about who the young man was to dismiss him. Instead, Lord Guo simply called for more double-fried fish, and the chatter in the hall resumed.

The banquet continued until the moon began to set, and Chih, listening as the guests made ready to depart, realized none of them were talking about the interruption at all. There were some significant looks exchanged and some lips pursed against gossip, and they were beginning to have some idea of the position that Lord Guo held.

It could be respect, I suppose, but fear's heavier and this feels like fear.

In the hustle to clear out the banquet hall, Chih hitched up their sleeves and gathered up a stack of plates. They were porcelain, far more precious than disposable earthenware, and they fell into step with the harried servants who were too busy to notice one more pair of hands.

"That was something with the lord's son," they mentioned to one of the servers, who turned out to be Five again. Five did a double-take, glaring when he recognized Chih.

"You sure do love your gossip, cleric."

"I do. I love it so much, and I hear so much of it that I can never remember who told me what. Usually that's my neixin's job, but she's away at the moment."

There was a little dip in their belly when they said it. It felt wrong, doing this without their best friend. They missed Almost Brilliant so much it was like a physical pain, but Five shrugged.

"Nothing to tell. Lord Guo's mad son. He got sick when he was five, and he's been like that ever since."

"Like that?"

"Refuses to wear proper clothes, sleeps all day, walks around all night. He bites people. There's a guard that doesn't work here anymore, he's missing the first joint on his middle finger because of Young Lord Guo."

"Have you met him personally?"

"Who hasn't? We have to bring him his meals and then we stand there as he checks it over to make sure that there's no meat in it, no bite of chicken or fish or pork. We can cook things in meat broth, and eggs are fine, but gods help us if there's a bite of meat. He takes his meals in the Jonquil Pavilion. That's where he lives if you're so desperate to have plates and food thrown at you."

Five's tone told Chih what he thought of that, and Chih nodded in appreciation as they deposited their stack of plates by the dish-washing station, a series of water troughs set up by the kitchen.

"Thank you for telling me how to get back to the guest pavilion," Chih said, their voice pitched to carry. "I've gotten so turned around."

"Don't mention it."

Chih wouldn't, and they slipped away, leaving the bustle and glow of the kitchens behind.

The spaces between the manor's pavilions were dark, and while there were the occasional bursts of noise from the servants' quarters or the guards calling to one another, there was a density to the quiet, something a little like anticipation, and they walked faster.

Chapter Four

Chih found themself awake in the full dark, sometime after the moon had set, completely alert without a wisp of sleep to carry them through to morning.

Shouldn't have fallen asleep under the willow today, they thought, and then they realized that they weren't the only one awake.

Silhouetted by the low light of the brazier, Nhung sat at the window, the shutters open to the night. Her dark hair was braided for sleep, and in her apricot silk sleeping robe, there was something dreamlike about her. Then Chih looked again, and no, she was just a girl restless after meeting her prospective husband, and she turned to Chih with wide eyes.

"You're awake," she whispered.

"So are you. We should probably both try to get back to sleep."

"No, I can't. Can we go out instead? My parents are

full of food and exhausted—they'll sleep through the day if we let them. Oh, Chih, please? I want to know this place. I must know this place."

Chih was about to say that they could get to know this place tomorrow, with a proper guide and in decent light, but Nhung came to them to take their hand, bringing it to her chest. She was warm through the thin silk of her robe, and under Chih's palm there was the rapid animal beat of her heart, far too fast.

"Just for a little while, all right? I don't want the guards to catch us out."

"Oh, the guards, no one cares about them," said Nhung scornfully. "Come on."

Chih put on their robe first, because it was usually an advantage to be recognized as a cleric, and they followed Nhung out the door, carefully avoiding the noisy steps by dropping directly to the ground. Chih picked up one of the small tin lanterns that stood by the door, lighting it with a taper, and they walked out into the night.

There was some commotion going on nearby, in a space still lit with lanterns and sheltered from view by frames hung with canvas. Chih and Nhung made a wide circuit around it, and soon they were in the depths of Doi Cao, what might have been as many as thirty buildings scattered along the paths with no direct way to any of them.

The only lights left were the soft lanterns that

burned at the doors of the inhabited buildings, lights for people who needed the latrines and to fend off the approach of the things that loved the darkness. In poorer houses, they would be made of paper, but here at Doi Cao they were colored glass, lighting the way with soft green, red, and blue.

Chih thought that Nhung wanted to talk. There was plenty that she might have wanted to talk about, but instead she took Chih's arm and they walked in silence, following the spiral path that circled the main manor and would, if followed, take them all the way to the outbuildings and the servants' sleeping quarters.

I wonder where on the spiral Jonquil Pavilion is, Chih thought, though they had their suspicions.

They paused at the pond, where some of the phosphorescent carp rose to the surface to investigate the glow of their tin lantern. The carp were small, but they lit up softly green on their backs and on the very tips of their whiskers. There was a craze for them in the east, Chih had heard, specially bred fish that glowed with mosaic patterns in the dark. They were delicate compared to the muddy breeds, and prone to illness, but the greater danger lay in predatory birds who liked a meal so invitingly visible in the dark.

"He said that they had been brought from the capital just like the cooks, the guards, and the house servants," Nhung mused. "They are quite far from home."

"But they have learned to live here," Chih offered. "They are safe, and happy, and comfortable."

Nhung laughed. "Oh, do you think I see myself in these poor things? Do not worry yourself, Cleric Chih. I like to eat carp, and I am at home wherever I have a full belly. Still, I wonder."

She did not elaborate what she wondered upon, and they continued on the spiral, stopping at a darkened building overgrown with vines. It had a faintly desolate air about it, but it wasn't until Chih breathed in an unnervingly familiar scent of rot that they stiffened.

"What is it?" asked Nhung, her hand tightening on their arm.

"Rotting paper," Chih said shortly, and they made their way to the building itself. It was locked, but the key hung from a nail on the porch post, and when they took it down, shreds of spiderwebs came with it. Chih cleaned it off with their sleeve, and then, on second thought, lifted the edge of their robe to cover their nose.

"You may want to cover your face or stand back."

"What evil spirits are you afraid of?" asked Nhung, half-joking, but Chih didn't smile in response.

"Mildew, mice, and silverfish, I'm afraid," Chih said, and opened the door.

They were met with a wave of wet, suffocating air, and if they could not see a plume of spores puff out towards their face, it was only because it was so dark.

The damp had set in as it liked to when archives were left too much to themselves, and the result was a dim room filled with moldering things that had once been important.

"What a mess," Chih said disconsolately, and Nhung stepped up to stand beside them, only to fall back again with a shudder.

"I suppose it used to be the library," Nhung said from the cleaner air.

"It smells as if no one has opened it in years."

"That may very well be the case. Lord Guo has been in residence for more than twenty years, and he has no interest in books or records beyond what his accountant keeps. This place belongs to the people who came before. What a shame, it looks as though it used to be quite splendid."

Chih gingerly picked up a volume that had fallen to the floor, a simple series of signatures bound in horse-hair without benefit of a cover. It had been sheltered somewhat from the rot that affected its fellows, but it breathed mold when they picked it up.

"Poor thing," Chih couldn't help saying, as they stepped back out into the porch. "But see, it's salvage-able, perhaps."

"What would you do to salvage it?" asked Nhung, who stayed where she was on the step.

"Me? Not much. I could cut the binding threads and lay out the pages to dry in the sun. Every city clerk knows to do that. Some of my friends back home, they would have shelves and shelves of tools and solvents and racks and presses to restore the records within. They wouldn't be happy about it, though."

"Hard to imagine anyone being happy with dealing with that mess. Come here."

Chih came down the steps to be folded into Nhung's arms, enveloped in silk and the smell of sleepy flesh. Her jasmine perfume had worn off almost entirely, leaving her with a vital animal smell that Chih liked better.

"I'm really fine," they mumbled.

"You didn't see your face. But you will be fine. And if I become the lady here, we'll fix it, all right? We'll surely be able to afford people to come and rescue your books."

"That would be wonderful. They're probably just household accounts and housekeeper journals, things like that, but you never know if there's something wonderful there, something that should be kept."

"So earnest," Nhung teased. "Be careful I don't try to keep you too."

"Your very own tamed cleric, brought in feral from the highway," Chih said, finally laughing. "Your mother would love it."

"Oh, she won't mind once I'm properly married. This is all about me getting a husband and a household after all."

She sounded a little sad at the last, and Chih gave her a hug. Other people's sadness was always easier to care for than their own, and perhaps if Nhung did become the mistress of Doi Cao, she would let Chih or some other cleric from Singing Hills in to see what could be done about the library.

They tucked the damaged book into their robe, and with Nhung on their arm, they continued their nocturnal walk. In the woods beyond the wall, they could hear the occasional scream of a happy fox or a dying rabbit, and from time to time, there were the guards' calls from post to post.

Once they heard the heavy tread of a guard's boots, and Nhung pulled them behind the meditation stones in the garden. In the darkest part of the shadow, Chih's sleeve held up to cover their lantern, they watched the guard go by, so close they could have reached out to tap his shoulder or tip his peaked cap from his head. Chih had to press their hand over their mouth at the hilarity of it, and when he had passed by, they did break into laughter.

"Oh, we really shouldn't," Chih said through their laughter. "We're not children—"

"I'm only a silly girl," Nhung said gravely. "Aren't I a child until I get married, when I shall magically become the lady of the house? Until then, anyway, I'm a child with silly whims, and you have to indulge me."

"Of course I do," Chih said, and they walked on.

There were many buildings that made up the Doi Cao estate. Some of them were enormous and impressive, like the main hall, the armory, and the primary residence of Lord Guo, but others were far more humble despite their grandiose names. Big or small, they all intrigued Nhung, and she ran up the pathways to their doors as eagerly as if they were sweetshops or booksellers. They could not budge the doors of the larger buildings, but the smaller ones had keys hung up beside the doors or were left unlocked entirely.

"But you must go first," Nhung insisted. "What if something terrible came out of the darkness to attack me?"

"It should attack me instead?" Chih asked wryly, but they didn't mind. If they were being entirely honest with themself, there was an illicit thrill in their night haunting. There was nothing as much fun as getting to go where they weren't supposed to, and even if they were only entering dusty storerooms full of gardening equipment or old lawn decorations, it was still a thrill.

It wasn't until Cloud Cat Cottage, a lovely little place with a decorative apple tree in front, that Chih actually found something ugly waiting for them. Seated in a niche like the one where they had found the spider at Eighth Peony Pavilion, there was a small ceramic grotesque about the size of Chih's hand. It was an irregular thing with three squat limbs and a long gracile fourth arm that bent upwards to hook behind its head, pulling back the loose skin of its face to reveal its eyes. There was a slight musty smell that came from the small holes punched in its back, and when Chih turned it over, they found a cork plug to keep the herbs inside.

"Look, isn't this the most hideous—"

Nhung flinched back from it, gagging and retreating down the stairs.

"Oh, awful. Oh, evil. Chih, doesn't it smell like the library to you?"

Now that she mentioned it, it did, that despairing odor of rot and neglect. Chih had to breathe through their mouth for a moment to get their breath.

"Throw it away, what an ugly thing."

Chih started to pitch it into the pond nearby, but they paused, blinking.

"I'm really not sure I should. This doesn't belong to me."

"Oh. Well, I suppose that's fair," Nhung said dubiously. "But perhaps you could at least empty out whatever's gone so foul inside? It must have gone bad. That smells so terrible, it will make us both sick. Really, it smells just like the library."

Holding the little figurine in their hand, Chih gagged again, and they hurriedly removed the plug. A dusting of dried herbs blew away when they upended it in the garden, and Nhung sighed with relief.

"This house does not take care of its old buildings," she said disapprovingly, coming to stand next to Chih.

"I think they were trying to, though," said Chih, peering at the ceramic figurine in their hand. "It looks a bit like the slithering beasts on the roof, doesn't it?"

"Perhaps a bit."

Nhung gingerly touched the ceramic figurine with a fingertip, so nervous that Chih almost thought it might reach out and bite her. When it lay dormant in Chih's hand, Nhung smiled, taking it from them.

"What a silly thing. Do you know, I almost like it now? Show me where it was."

Nhung replaced it in its niche in the pavilion, looking around curiously.

"Why, this must have been for a baby, don't you think?"

Lifting their lantern higher, Chih could see that it was. The screens were painted with sweet frolicking rabbits and chickens, and the chests containing the bedding for the room were carved with a motif of little children running after a ball. In the corner, there was a tilted stool with a long back where a nursemaid could sit as she fed the baby. Nhung crossed immediately to the chair, dropping down on it.

"I'll feed my own babies here," she declared. "I insist upon it."

"You should make that part of your marital contract," Chih said, coming to sit beside her on the ground. "If you don't, the choice is your lord's."

"Of course it is." Nhung rolled her eyes. "What stupid rules."

Chih started to tell her that perhaps she could change them if she became the lady of Doi Cao when a light briefly shone through the cracked door. Both Chih and Nhung froze, watching as the light lingered and then moved on.

"Another guard," Chih murmured, but Nhung shook her head.

"Not so soon after the last, not even if they staggered their patrols to catch unwary thieves."

She slipped from the chair to the ground, moving silently on her hands and knees until she could peer through the door.

"Oh! Why, it's Guo Zhihao."

"Who?"

"The young lord. The uninvited one at the feast."

There was a fascinated tone in her voice, and before Chih could call her back, she was out the door, moving as soundlessly as a cloud over the moon. Chih wavered a moment, but then they followed her into the dark shadows of the decorative statues in the garden, watching as the slender figure of Guo Zhihao reeled along the spiral path.

The first time they had met him, he had been full of scorn, and the second time, he had been furious. This time, he moved with a faltering step, his arms hanging woodenly down by his sides and his head jerked up towards the sky as if there was a string running from his chin to the rooftops.

Instinctively, Chih looked up, following his gaze, but all they found was sky itself, the revolution of the stars interrupted only by the flight of bats.

"Oh, he's beautiful," Nhung said in a way that meant no good, or at least, no peace. "Chih, don't you think he's beautiful?"

There was something striking about the young lord, clad in his sleeping robes and barefoot, but instead it struck a brass drum inside Chih's ear, sending a tremolo of unease down their back.

"Very attractive," they said. "But Nhung, perhaps we should—"

Nhung moved quickly and silently from their shelter under the statue of the mountain goddess to the lee of a box hedge, and Chih, not wishing to be left behind, caught hold of the trailing edge of her sleeve to keep up.

"Nhung!"

"Shh," Nhung said, not looking back. "He'll belong to me when I am lady here, won't he? I'll be his mother."

"You do not sound very motherly right now," Chih said urgently, because a girlish urge to explore her new home was one thing—being caught in her sleeping clothes with her new husband's son was another.

"Of course I do. I sound very motherly and concerned. He might catch his death."

She sounded so certain that Chih nearly believed her, but she was watching the young lord with such wide and fascinated eyes that the only person Nhung was fooling was herself, and that probably only poorly.

"Nhung, we should return to Eighth Peony. We could be in a great deal of trouble."

Nhung started to turn, annoyed, but Zhihao reeled on his feet, stumbling over some irregularity in the path. He managed to catch himself before he fell, but it was a near thing, especially as he didn't put his arms out for balance.

"Why, he's sleepwalking," Nhung said, fascinated. "Oh, Chih, but he could harm himself if he were allowed to keep on. Surely we cannot let that happen, can we?"

Chih thought of the ponds that dotted the Doi Cao estate, how slippery the banks and the rocks were. They were lovely, but they were also deceptively deep, giving the carp that lived in them places to hide.

"We shouldn't," they said reluctantly, and Nhung smiled in triumph.

"Come on, we shall see him settled, and then, I promise, we can return to bed like good little children."

Before Chih could make a response to that, Nhung had whisked her sleeve out of their fingers, trotting after Zhihao as if it was quite decided. Chih frowned, wavered, and then followed.

"You are away from your bed, little lord," Nhung was saying softly. "You have gone wandering in the night, and there are things abroad that do not love you, that wish to eat you."

Zhihao stopped to look at Nhung in his path, his head tilted and his mouth working around soundless words. Chih wasn't sure what he was seeing, but there was only a small chance it was Nhung.

"Young Lord Guo, we should return you to your bed," Chih said soothingly, but Nhung shook her head.

"Of course we can't. His keepers will be there, and then everyone will know where we've been. No, come, my little lord. I know a place."

When he would not give her his hand, she took him by the tie of his robe instead and, like a cow on a rope, she led him back to the nursery. At Nhung's direction, Chih opened up one of the chests to pull out some carefully packed bedding, a pallet and a pillow stuffed with horsehair as well as a woven blanket. With gentle words and a little bit of tugging, she got the young lord settled in, resting on his back with his arms still woodenly locked by his sides.

"They used to call sleepwalking being fox-led," Chih murmured, closing the chest and coming to sit next to Nhung. "They used to say that a fox would lead someone out of bed and confuse them so badly they would never find their way home."

"What a terrible story," Nhung said, smoothing Zhihao's hair back from his face. In that moment, she did look maternal, tender enough to cry over the young man who lay there with his eyes half-open. "You must not tell it again, for surely it will frighten people who do not know it is only a restless mind and an upset spirit that sends people wandering in their sleep."

Chih started to respond, but Zhihao turned his head towards their voices.

"Get out," he said, his voice soft and high. When he had spoken to them in the yard and again when he had spoken in the banqueting hall, his voice was the tenor of a healthy young man. Now it was cracked like a plate, the voice of a child, and Nhung made a soft sympathetic sound.

"Poor thing. Poor lovely thing. It's all right. We're here. We're here, and we will not let you come to harm."

"Get out," Zhihao pleaded. "They're not in Shu. They're not in Shu, they are—"

He choked, convulsing momentarily before lying still.

There was a fine sweat on his brow despite the midnight cool, and in close quarters, there was a clear chemical note to his scent. It was something like the smell apothecaries got, a sharp herbal odor that clung to their sleeves, but in Zhihao there was something musky to it as well, a smell of closed rooms and medicine balls wrapped in sugar tissue to make them easier to bear.

"Here, poor thing, I will press my lips to your forehead, and that will soothe you. My nurse did the same for me, and it put me to sleep right away."

Nhung leaned down over her knees, and where Chih thought the smell would turn her away, she only did as she said, pressing her lips to his forehead. It came to Chih how wonderfully cool her lips would be against fevered skin, how it would be both a relief and a blessing, and the shiver of jealousy that ran through their body was so foreign that it made them blink.

Now Nhung sat up, running an absent tongue over her teeth.

"Poor thing," she repeated, but now at least the young lord lay still, a marginally more peaceful look on his face. In the lantern light, his eyes were still open, just a sliver of darkness against the night, but the tension had gone out of his body, and his hands were open and soft.

Finally, Nhung rose from Zhihao's side, smoothing her hands down her sleeping robes as if they were the finest court attire.

"We should return to Eighth Peony," she said as if it was a brand-new idea, and relieved, Chih let her lead the way.

It was not dawn yet, but there was a certain lightness to the sky that said it was not far off. Somewhere close by, a bird called out, a loud and hollow whistle that started low, rose two notes, and dropped again.

"A pearl thrush," Chih murmured. "In Zhou, they say it is the sun's child and it respectfully greets its mother with every dawn."

"Do they?" asked Nhung absently. "Where we come from, it sings because it is grateful it was not eaten in the night. I would sing for that too."

Eighth Peony was silent when they returned. They removed their shoes on the walk, and remembering the steps, they boosted themselves up straight onto the deck and slid the door open. The elder Phams were still asleep as they went past, Madame Pham sprawled like a rag doll over her husband's chest and both snoring loudly enough that Chih could see that they needn't have worried about the stairs.

Nhung leaned over them affectionately as she passed. For a moment, it almost looked as if she was going to stroke their heads, and then she brought her mother's robe up more securely around her shoulders and patted her father's hand.

"We're a little less formal in my household," she said, embarrassed. "I should remember myself now that I am going to be a lady."

"Different ways for different households," said Chih with a shrug.

"I don't want to be a silly little girl pretending to be a great lady," she mumbled, and they cuddled together on her pallet. She seemed heavier suddenly, as if the weight of her worry made her dense, and she burrowed against Chih's shoulder. "They'll laugh at me."

"Let me tell you a story," Chih said. "Will that make you feel better?"

"Always. Tell me one about a girl who comes to a great house and charms the lord of the manor so well he immediately gives it to her so that all her family will be safe and happy forever."

"What a good story. All right. Once, when the rocks and stones were still soft . . ."

Chapter Five

Chih woke up far too soon to the sounds of excited chatter in the pavilion. For one confused moment, they wondered how the thrushes from the night before had gotten inside, but then they woke up further and realized it was the chirping of little children.

That was hardly less out of place, so they dressed quickly and came around the screen to the table, where Nhung sat between two little girls with their hair braided into coils and dressed in silk robes dyed in a perfect gradation of orange to pink. On a platter before her were halved white peaches, the pits removed and the centers filled with a confection of pureed red beans and crystallized sugar. The elder Phams sat at the head of the table side by side, watching the goings-on with pleasure.

"Chih, come sit down and try the breakfast Lord Guo has sent to us! My little fairies were just telling me how it is in the Flower-Fruit Kingdom, where this all came from."

Each of the little girls had a peach for their own, and their faces were sticky with juice and sugar as they talked over one another, describing a land where sugar water ran in the streams and candied hawthorn grew in skewers on the bank like cattails. They fairly buzzed like bees, and Chih was pleased not to be in charge of them. They took a small bite from one of the peaches, and as they guessed, it was so sweet it made their teeth tingle.

"It's good," they said, and they turned to see what Almost Brilliant would make of it with her bird's palate before they remembered she wasn't with them. They realized they had been missing her a great deal this trip, and they started to say so when the stairs sang and a young page appeared at the door.

"Lord Guo hopes that you have taken pleasure and delight from the emissaries of the Flower-Fruit Kingdom that he sent to you this morning. He further states that if my lady would like to behold the home of these mythical beings, she should come with me to the garden."

The elder Phams cried out with delight, lifting their daughter up and ready to rush her out in her sleeping robes. Nhung, laughing, shook them off.

"Come help me dress, cleric. I can hardly run off

to the Flower-Fruit Kingdom in my sleeping clothes, can I?"

She shooed her parents to the porch, where their exclamations over the generosity of Lord Guo could be heard from inside the cottage, and she pulled out her makeup box, her little bronze mirror, and her horn comb. She handed the comb to Chih with an admonition not to pull while she busied herself with her face powder.

Chih examined the comb with interest. It was a lovely antique with a perforated spine, twisting smooth lines with the curves cut out so that the comb could be strung on a cord and hung where the owner would be sure to find it every morning. The design had a sinuous grace to it, too worn to be recognized, but calling to mind the Ku Dynasty fashions around them.

A faint scent rose up from Nhung's hair with each pass, her signature jasmine oil and the darker smell of Nhung herself underneath. Chih had to resist the urge to bury their face in it, straightening up and blushing slightly at the impulse.

"You know, I'm really not a lady's maid."

"I told you, she ran off to join the circus," Nhung said absently, painting a three-petaled flower at the center of her forehead. The design was not much larger than a cherry, and she picked up an even finer brush to give it pistils and leaves.

"Which circus?" Chih asked, because Almost Brilliant would have wanted them to, and Nhung shot them an amused look over her bare shoulder.

"The one with the tightrope walkers and the women breathing fire and the dark-skinned mermaid in the glass vessel, of course," she said. "Tell me I look beautiful."

"You look very beautiful," Chih said, and they helped Nhung get into her robes.

The outermost robe was done up in a gorgeous pink raw silk, and the robe beneath it was a demure silver silk that sparkled like a bright morning drizzle, but the underrobes were only a light cotton, and one, Chih suspected, was woven from hemp thread, coarse and lumpen.

"I'm the most terrible kind of fake," Nhung said when they caught Chih rubbing the fabric between their thumb and forefinger, and she looked so tremulously brave that Chih took her hand in theirs to squeeze it.

"Not at all. You are a real person who is going into a real future."

They were escorted on the spiral path to the area that had been curtained and lit up the night before. Now the screens had been taken down to reveal a carefully crafted, beautifully realized garden of sugar and almonds. The small ornamental trees had been groomed to a nicety, and the branches were studded with dried berries glazed with sugar to make them shine. When Nhung tried to pluck one of the peonies, it shattered in her hand, the petals made of pink sugar paste breaking off to tumble to the floor.

"How lovely," Nhung said, looking around, and Chih smiled, though they might have added *how expensive* or *how exhausting.* This, then, probably explained the harried kitchen workers and the baleful glares. The Flower-Fruit Kingdom was gorgeous, but it was more sugar than any one person could eat, and as the sun rose higher, the sugar would start to sweat. By noon, it would be a sticky mess, and there was a reason this sort of exhibition had fallen out of favor in the capital.

At the center of all of this sat Lord Guo, his face wreathed in a wide smile and his hands open as if he would like to take all the world into his grasp.

"A beauty for a beauty," he said, and Chih wondered how often he had said those words.

Nhung blushed becomingly and went to him, her parents on either side practically pushing her along. She took a gingerish seat on his knee, and when she opened her mouth to thank him, he pressed a scrolled sugar leaf into it.

A pair of young women in the same robes worn by the little girls stepped forward, arm in arm, to sing her a song written for the occasion, and Chih took the distraction to ease away into the background and then out of the sugar garden entirely.

It'll be fine, they thought. *There are plenty of descriptions of sugar gardens in the records, and if there aren't, I'll just pick up a culinary magazine on my way back through Anh. However, it looks as if most of the household is here, and if everyone is here—*

As they guessed, Jonquil Pavilion was located close to the walls, pressed right up against the brick. It lacked the fluted eaves and graceful porches of the other buildings, and far from having singing stairs, the house had front steps of plain board set over block risers.

The guard at the door gave Chih a wary look as they approached.

"The young lord is not taking visitors."

Before Chih could decide how they wanted to convince the guard otherwise, a voice came from the depths of the house.

"Who is that on the step?"

"No one, young lord."

"Liar!" The word was flung like a stone, and Chih and the guard, who they could see now was very young, winced.

"The Phams' cleric, young lord."

"Let them in."

"Young lord, I—"

Zhihao erupted into curses, more sailor than scholar.

"Let them in!"

His shout was accompanied by a crash of breaking glass, and the guard gave Chih a disgusted look.

"Be careful, cleric. He bites."

Chih climbed the stairs to Jonquil Pavilion, sliding aside the door to be confronted with darkness. The window shutters were all bolted shut, and there were screens set up immediately inside the entrance. Jonquil Pavilion was large, but a multitude of screens divided it again and again until it was a dim maze of wood and fabric and paper.

"Come through," Zhihao called, a hint of anger in his voice. "There is only one path, as twisted as it is."

"Of course, young lord."

The way was narrow, a warren of old screens that must have been salvaged over time. Some were newer, showing off the court figures and poetical beauties that were currently in vogue, but the deeper Chih went, the older the screens became, revealing scenes from old stories and religious lessons all grayed with dust and occasionally torn through misuse.

At the heart of the labyrinth, there was a dim and flickering light, and seated behind it was Guo Zhihao, dressed in his sleeping robe and with his hair tied back in a tangle.

"Come and sit," he said. "You have come to stare, you might as well be comfortable."

Chih knelt down where he indicated, folding their hands on their lap before bowing over their knees.

"I have come to learn," they said, and Zhihao barked a quick harsh laugh, nothing funny in it.

"And what does a sick man have to teach you? I can tell you how poppy extract tastes when it is all you have drunk for three days. I can tell you that the restraints they brought from the capital for me are more comfortable than my old ones. What would you like to learn, cleric?"

"Those are all worthy things, but I am here to speak to you about what you said yesterday when the Phams' entourage arrived," said Chih as calmly as they could. The mention of restraints made their stomach turn over.

"I told you. Tell her to ask him how many wives he has had."

"There are many stories," Chih said meditatively, "of young wives being told to ask their husbands about this or that, opening up years of hurt and poison. I would not have Pham Nhung open up any such jars without good cause."

"And if there is hurt and poison there, cleric, isn't it better that she should know sooner rather than later what lies in the old storage rooms?"

Chih hesitated.

"I am Cleric Chih of Singing Hills, the archivists' order. I am here to learn and to mark down, and it seems to me—"

"A bird," Zhihao said abruptly. "A cleric of your order came through when I was very young. They had a bird, they said that all of their order did. Small and striped and bold, they forgot nothing. Where is your bird?"

"Almost Brilliant is—she's not with me right now, unfortunately. Still, I have been trained to remember as well in my own human way. Perhaps that will be enough?"

"Memory breaks, cleric, didn't you know? I would have liked to meet your bird."

"I wish you could meet her too. She's wonderful. But, tell me—"

"I can't."

Chih waited, and Zhihao's head jerked from side to side as if there were a fly buzzing around his head.

No, not a fly, a wasp, they thought, and a big one, judging by the fearful look on his face.

"I can't," he insisted. "I speak, and it comes, and it comes and it—"

His mouth snapped shut with an audible click, hard enough to chip enamel, and abruptly he lunged. Chih yelped, falling back against the screen, the memory of the guard missing a finger in their mind, but Zhihao was only reaching for a writing box beside them.

It was an elderly thing, battered and held together with brass tacks and a strip of glued leather, far too humble for a lord's son, but Zhihao's hands were on it like it was the last food in the world. He threw the lid up, removing small squares of paper that he thrust onto the floor. Instead of a brush and ink, he had a stick of graphite like the kind that Chih used themself, and he started to scrawl frantically on the sheets of paper.

"No, no, no," he growled through gritted teeth, and then the words cut off entirely as his jaw locked. In the silence, there was only the furious scrape of graphite on the fine linen paper and then a snap as the graphite broke and he threw half of it away in fury.

Instinctively, Chih reached over to calm him, but the young lord was growing increasingly agitated, a low whining snarl coming from between his locked teeth.

Page after page fluttered out from under his frantic scrawl, and page after page, he crumpled angrily, shoving them aside. Chih squinted to see what he was writing, and they crossed some invisible barrier. One moment Zhihao was focused entirely on the paper in front of him, and the next, he had reared up, shoving Chih away.

Chih squawked as they went over straight into one of the screens, sending it to the floor with a deafening clatter, and then Zhihao was on them, his hands batting at Chih furiously.

Oh, I have made some choices, Chih thought blankly, fending him off. They flailed, looking for anything they could use to defend themself, but they only came up with paper, paper, and more paper, a veritable field's worth of drifting chaff.

There was shouting and a terrible crash, more screens coming down, and then there was a man grabbing hold of Zhihao, dragging him back. Even in his shouted orders, there was a kind of exasperated experience to the way he pinned Zhihao's arms behind him at a painful angle, but something today went wrong. With what looked like a titanic effort, Zhihao broke free with a cry only for his jaws to lock again with a toothbreaking snap. Loose, he was on Chih again, his hands reaching and clawing like the talons of some digging animal, and Chih tried ineffectually to stiff-arm him away before he was lifted bodily off of them, this time thrust to the floor and smothered underneath his own mattress.

Something about the image, Zhihao pushed howling to the floor under the suffocating weight of his own bedding, the weight of the guard smashing him flat, made Chih want to throw up.

"Don't, oh don't," they cried, and the guard spared them an angry look.

"You agitated him enough, now leave. See what you have done."

Zhihao shrieked loud enough that Chih's throat ached in sympathy, and the guard pushed down harder.

"Get out, or it will only be the worse for him!"

Chih fled the scene, because they could only imagine

how much worse it might go, and they were met at the door by another guard and a well-dressed woman carrying a wooden box on a strap over her shoulder. She flinched at the sounds coming from Jonquil Pavilion.

"You must go," she said to Chih. "He's well past reason now."

Reaching into her box, she pulled out a cloudy glass bottle, tipping the reeking contents into a cloth. Even from a distance, the fumes stung Chih's nose and mouth, and they gagged as the woman and the guard ran into the house.

They listened as there was one final shriek and then an uncanny, skincrawling silence. Biting their lip, they circled the house, coming at last to a window that had been propped open. Through the window, despite the drapes and the screens, Chih could hear scraps of conversation from within.

"—agitated ever since he heard that his father was marrying again—"

"—should keep him down until the wedding—"

"—keep everyone *out,* I told you both. Twelve hells, I keep telling you, don't I."

Chih made their way back to Eighth Peony, which, in the absence of the Phams, was desolate, the ruin of the sugared delicacies from the morning sweating pink and green and purple onto the table. Chih picked at the scraps with a shaking finger. The almond paste was a cloying weight on their tongue and their throat, and they managed to swallow it mostly by reminding themself that it was rare and expensive rather than because they actually liked it.

"That was a curse, wasn't it?" they asked the empty room. "Someone called for a sorcerer and had them bind his tongue. If he speaks, it will choke him, and if he persists, it will kill him. And perhaps they will one day suffocate him under his own mattress, and call it an accident."

Almost Brilliant might have been able to tell them what curse it was, what type of sorcerer from which cult might have cast it, but Almost Brilliant wasn't there, and they missed her so terribly they burst into tears. It was an intense squall, if a brief one, and they wiped their eyes with surprise.

How strange. I'm not usually given to tears, am I?

They stood and resolutely began tidying. Singing Hills always said that if you could not have a tidy mind, you could at least have a tidy room. When they were young, they had thought it was just an excuse to keep the novices cleaning, but right then, they would take any clarity they could get.

When the salvageable sweets had been packed away and the paper all set out for burning, they lit the little brazier to heat some water. There was a canister of tea the staff had left for the guests, but they went into their own bags instead, coming up with a light muslin bag of dried and rolled tea leaves.

Set to steep in the teapot they took down from its niche, the tea produced was a deep ochre-red with a strong flavor of metal. It was bracing to sit down and sip it from their tin traveling cup rather than one of the porcelain cups that were set so perfectly on a side table. It was good and harsh, and they poured themself another cup from the teapot, patting its curved side in appreciation. It was a startlingly homely object for the Phams, orange speckled with a white and black glaze, perhaps an antique or a childhood indulgence of Nhung's.

It came to Chih to draw it, and they went looking in their things again to find paper and graphite only to come up with the damaged book they had taken from the moldering library the night before. In their hands now, it seemed like they had smuggled it out of a dream, something not properly real.

I should put it back, they thought, because damaged or not it belonged to Lord Guo, but instead they went around to the porch behind the cottage, locating a particularly bright spot that would catch the sunlight. With their knife, they split the cords holding the signatures together and spread them out, taking pebbles from the garden to weigh them down. Sunlight was terrible for books, but used briefly, it would dry out the black blooms of mold. Then the mold could be brushed away and Chih could see what other repairs the book might need.

They spread the pages out carefully, noting that it was no household account or housekeeper log at all, but a volume about the history of the slithering beasts on the roof.

In the final years of the Ku Dynasty, the empire was eaten from within by rich bureaucrats and from without by strange beasts. These beasts, it seemed to me, walked in darkness and in the high places and the low ones, as sly as the scarf of a dancing girl trailed over an unwary nape, as deadly as poison offered by a friend or a lover.

The accompanying picture was marred by water damage, eaten past easy recognition, but the more Chih stared at it, the more vivid it became, the image of a long-limbed, long-snouted animal undulating along the slope of a roof, the spangles of mold giving it depth and menace.

They turned away, the mold making them feel light-headed and a little sick to their stomach. Another cup of tea calmed them, and they knelt at the table, thinking again to draw the little calico teapot. Instead, their mind wandered, and when they looked down, they had drawn a hoopoe instead: Almost Brilliant, with her pert head, the sharp blades of her wings and the fan of her tail. They smiled to see her before reaching into their robe for more paper, but then they blinked. They had put no paper into their robe, but there it was. Apprehension prickled the back of their neck, and nervously, they pulled out the paper that had been slid between their robe and their undergarments, held in place by their belt. The paper was far finer than what they used, thick and toothy and stiff enough to stand on its own when they held it between thumb and forefinger. They remembered the young lord's hands like frantic flying birds, desperate to send a message, and now, he had.

They smoothed the crumpled paper out on the table, half-expecting it to be a meaningless scribble. Some of the lockjaw curses were like that, the powerful ones capable of eroding the very ability to speak or write if they were not undone. Almost Brilliant would have known which ones were that powerful, but Chih couldn't think of her just then.

At first it looked like nothing more than a graphite scrawl, but then, from the chaos there emerged a set of crooked characters, written so sloppily they lay on their fronts or their backs rather than standing upright. Chih had to turn the paper over and over again to figure out what the smudged and broken lines indicated, and then they knew.

Graceful Fin Cottage. Moonset.

"Well, that's very interesting," said Nhung from the doorway. "You must tell me everything."

Chapter Six

There was another banquet that night, featuring fire-eaters and tumblers from the west. Chih heard a passing server whisper that the negotiations for Nhung's hand must be going well—Lord Guo hadn't had fire-eaters since the lady from Kirshan. Which lady was that, another server wanted to know, but they were both fiercely shushed and Chih learned no more.

From behind their screen, they watched as Lord Guo fed Nhung by hand, already foolish fond. He looked like he would prove an indulgent husband, giving her the best of everything off his plate, but Chih also saw that he would insist. Even if Nhung did not care for the finest morsels, she would be forced to eat them, or at least, it was difficult to imagine such a big man being balked in such a trivial matter. Far better to give him what he wanted when it was so easy, wasn't it? On such things marriages were founded, Cleric

Sun back at the abbey had said disapprovingly. They had left their own marriage in a fiery ruin and gone to sea. Nhung only hesitated a moment, making some half-hearted protest of not liking mushrooms before she opened her mouth.

There was no interruption that night, but there was no great crowd either. Only the wealthiest of the local families were in attendance, and they brought with them gifts of food and of incense. If the negotiations continued to go well, the third and final night would see only the most important men in the district with the most impressive gifts, and Lord Guo and Pham Nhung would be married before them.

The banquet went on into the night, long after Nhung herself had pled off for weariness and over-excitement. Chih took her arm to lead her away, and they were conscious briefly of Lord Guo's considering gaze before Madame Pham, enjoying the plum wine very much, stood up and declared that she would sing for all assembled.

"Oh, when I was a little girl, I was so beautiful that the fish jumped out of the water into my mouth, and none of my siblings ever went hungry! Let me sing to you of how beautiful I was!" she cried as Master Pham tried to pull her back down to her seat.

Nhung made a face as they departed.

"Mother comes from humble origins. She tries not

to let on. She wants so much better for me, even as happy as she is with Father."

"I'm certainly not going to fault her for it. Though perhaps she'd like to sing me that song. I'm not sure I've heard it before."

"You must not," said Nhung sternly. "She's sensitive. Promise me you won't."

"I promise," said Chih, and Nhung looped her arm through theirs, friends again.

"And anyway, we have more important things to think of. We should sleep, I think, until moonset."

"I sleep pretty deeply. I may not be able to wake up if I'm sleeping well."

Nhung's eyes went soft and dark, the way they had been when she saw Zhihao reeling down the path the night before.

"I'll be awake," she said softly, and she was, shaking Chih's shoulder until they rolled out of their blankets and, yawning, went out onto the porch to dress.

"Come on. Do you remember where Graceful Fin was? Was it one of the buildings we went to last night?"

"Um, I don't know," Chih said, rubbing their eyes. "I can't imagine it's one of the ones near the main buildings. Let's walk the spiral. We're sure to find it sooner or later."

The stars were out in force that night, but the moon was dropping rapidly into his bed. The path grew dimmer and dimmer, and by the time they found Graceful Fin Cottage, the path was almost invisible, evidenced only by the feel of stone under their shoes instead of grass or dirt. By the light of their lantern, Chih read *Graceful Fin* on the tablet in front of a cottage close to the wall.

"This is the place," Chih said, and Nhung took their arm, looking up at the cottage with dark worried eyes.

"Oh, it looks so eerie," she said. "Will you go in ahead and see if he is in there? I'll hide here until you tell me it's all right. And—"

"And keep an eye out for ugly things as well. I will," Chih said with a sigh. It was faintly irritating, Nhung's delicacy, but they wondered if there was something to it. They had dumped out several of the little ceramic figurines in their wanderings the night before, and at strange times, the scent of the dried herbs inside came back to them, musty and mildewed like the poor library.

They mounted the stairs and drummed their fingers on the doorframe, hopefully something that would be easily heard inside but not out. When there was no response, they slid the door open, and sneezed, because the smell was here again too, thick and cloying.

They swiftly found the little ceramic figurine, dumping the contents into the yard, but when they went to replace it, a hand fell on their shoulder.

"Oh, son of a—!"

They bit off a curse as Zhihao reached down to catch the ceramic figure that leaped out of their hand, saving it just inches from the floor.

"What in the world are you doing?" he asked, and they put their hand over their heart to still its rabbit beat.

"It's for Nhung," they wheezed. "She can't stand the smell."

By the light of Chih's taper, Zhihao's face creased with irritation.

"There's no smell," he said, replacing the figurine in its niche. "Where is she?"

"Outside. Let me call her."

Chih went to the door and slid it open just in time for Nhung to come straight through in a rustle of pomegranate silk. She moved with a cautious step, taking hold of Chih's arm again, but she regarded Zhihao with a calm and level look.

"Why did you bite off that guard's finger?" she asked.

Zhihao's grin was a sickle of sharpened bone.

"When something is put in my mouth, it becomes mine," he said, and Nhung laughed.

"That's what my mother always told me. Why have you called us here?"

Zhihao winced, and as Chih watched, the left corner of his mouth jerked up and then down as if someone had hooked a finger there and yanked. For a brief moment, they could see the shine of his teeth and his gums, and then he shook his head hard.

"Don't ask me that," he said. "Don't ask me anything."

"Oh, your poor mouth," Nhung murmured. She raised her hand to touch Zhihao's face, but he shied back from her, shaking his head.

"Don't touch me either," he insisted. "We're short on time. I'm meant to be passed out in my bed."

"They drugged you this afternoon," Chih said, remembering, and he shot them a sardonic glance.

"It was Madame Kuou. She's not very careful, only waits until I go limp. Still, I should thank her. When Madame Bi does it, I see ghosts for hours after I wake up. Come on."

Graceful Fin was a storage house, stacked high with rows of chests that left only narrow aisles to walk through. Nhung was thin and Zhihao just barely shy of emaciated, but Chih had to go sideways.

He led them to a cleared area in the back, and then, starting in one corner, he started taking down the chests to open them. The first five were winter furs, the spiky black of mink, the grizzled gray of wolf, and once the rare pale gold fur of a lynx. Zhihao flipped through each chest quickly, his fingers digging gingerly through the contents before replacing them in the stack.

"What are you looking for?" asked Nhung.

He glanced at her, not bothering to reply as whatever snagged the left side of his mouth now caught the right as well, tugging hard enough to give him a terrible grin. Chih and Nhung both winced as his lower lip split, sending a needle-thin stream of blood down his chin.

"Can we help?" asked Chih carefully, and this time, his smile was real, if pained.

"Yes. You'll know it when you see it."

The curse allowed him that, and he dabbed carelessly at the blood on his face with the sleeve of a chinchilla stole before he replaced it in the chest.

The three of them worked methodically, shifting the chests between them. Once or twice, the chests were locked, and when they were, Zhihao would simply shrug, bashing the mechanism with a small steel pick he produced from his robes.

"I'm the heir," he said after the first time he did it. "This is all mine."

There was no joy in the statement for him, though many people would have been grateful to inherit even a tenth of the wealth that they found in those chests. There was no gold or silver, no cash or deeds. Instead it was the material wealth of the house, the ceramics, textiles, and decorative objects that turned Doi Cao from an old compound in the backlands to a true estate. As they searched, Chih was startled by the quality of the goods uncovered. It was enough to outfit another house entirely, if not two, and all of it packed away out of the light.

"Oh, what a shame that this is not on display," Nhung murmured, echoing Chih's thoughts.

She pulled out a length of scarlet silk embroidered with gold thread. When she spread out just one end, it was revealed to be a wall hanging, depicting the marriage of the scholar and the tiger queen, each stitch delicate and evocative.

"When I rule here, I will be sure to hang it up so that everyone can see how beautiful it is. Such things should not be kept in the dark."

"You will never rule here, no matter who you marry," said Zhihao. There was no recrimination in his tone, only the simple cold statement of a fact he knew better than he knew his own face.

"Why do you say that?" asked Nhung.

"Who rules over a wealthy house but a man? Father, lord, or husband, no one else."

"There are many ways to rule," Nhung said with confidence, and they continued to look.

Twice, they had to go still and quiet for the watchmen who passed by, and Chih crouched down to hide their lantern in the deepest shadows. They had made their way through perhaps half the boxes when Chih pulled out one chest of pungent cedar. There was nothing to mark the chest from the rest, nothing in particular at all that should have made them wary, but Chih paused, a chill like a dead woman's fingertip running up their spine.

"Um," they said.

As Zhihao and Nhung turned to look, they took a deep breath and raised the lid. It came to them later that it hadn't been locked. What carelessness, but if Lord Guo had enough money to create a wonderland of sugar, to bring an entire household from the city to western Ji, to buy Pham Nhung, he had enough to be careless.

At first, they thought it was one more chest of furs. The cedar would bar the insects, and there was a scatter of small discs glued to the top, pieces of wool felt soaked with something sharp and astringent to keep away the mold.

The fur on top was fox, red and gold and white, but there was black as well, though less well preserved as it seemed clotted and dull with salt, and instead of fur, it was hair, and Chih fell back from the chest, clamping their hands over their mouth in horror.

"Ah, there we are," said Zhihao with a kind of terrible satisfaction, and he flipped back the fox fur to show a wizened face that still had all her teeth. Such white teeth they were, long now that the lips had pulled back with the disgust of the dead, and her hair lay in such dark clouds around her head, and Nhung screamed, short and sharp like the bark of some mortally wounded animal.

It was loud enough that Zhihao reached over to clamp his hand over her mouth and then he had to swallow a cry because she bit his hand hard enough that Chih saw blood flying. The sight of blood made them shudder—what if it fell on her? What if living blood fell on that terrible dead face, what then?—and it gave them the strength to shut the lid on the fox fur and the face of Lord Guo's wife.

They retreated back to the corners of the cleared space, Zhihao nursing his hand, Nhung rocking back and forth with her hands over her mouth, and Chih staring at both of them because if they didn't, they would be staring at the box, their curiosity like a well-trained dog leading them back to look again. They would see that it was exactly what it looked like, like someone had folded up a dead woman in fox furs and laid her in the chest.

"She's not in Shu," Chih said, their voice too high, and Zhihao nodded, his lips pressed together.

"Why would he do that?" Nhung moaned. "Why would he do that, she's dead, she's dead."

"Because he rules here," said Chih, coming to a decision. "All right. We need to clean up."

They could hardly believe it was their own voice, calm and smooth with only a trace of a waver.

"What are you going to do, cleric?" asked Zhihao.

He looked like a ghost himself in the darkness, gaunt in his sleeping clothes. He looked a bit like he had been dead as long as the woman in the trunk—and where were the others, Chih wondered—and no surprise, if this was the house he lived in. He fell into his fits at five, the cook's apprentice had said, and where was his mother then, except not in Shu? Dead or not, there was something in his face that was almost hopeful, and they tried to smile at him.

"Something smart, I hope," Chih said. "Leave. Tell someone. Send help for you as fast as possible. Nhung, we're leaving tomorrow, all right?"

Nhung was still staring at the chest as if at any moment the woman inside would lift the lid, crawling out trailing her fox fur. Chih shook her by the shoulder, and then knelt down deliberately between her and the chest, taking her by the arms.

"Pham Nhung, I need you to look at me, all right? What's my name?"

For a moment, Nhung only seemed to stare straight through them, but then, thankfully, she focused.

"Why, you're Cleric Chih."

"Very good! And where did we meet?"

"You. You dropped your books all over the road, and I helped you gather them."

"Of course you did. All right. And you trust me, don't you?

"Yes. Yes, I trust you."

"Good. And that means we need to return to Eighth Peony, and when you wake up tomorrow, you are going to be terribly, terribly sick, all right? So sick they have to send you home."

Nhung laughed. It came out high and piercing, but she clamped her own hand to her lips, biting down so hard that blood welled around her sharp teeth. It must have hurt terribly, but no sound escaped, and Chih slowly worked her hand out of her mouth.

"I am meant to be married tomorrow."

"Not if we're clever. Not if we're lucky," Chih insisted. "Almost Brilliant and I have gotten out of worse things. Come on. Come help me put everything back. One step at a time, that's how to do it, all right? Just one step."

Silently the three of them restacked the chests, and taking a deep breath, Chih did open the terrible chest again, examining the body within. She had been buried in natron, they realized, so she was as light and hollow as a pine liquor dream. She did not stain the fox furs that she rested upon, but instead the fur billowed up around her, lending her their color in place of her own.

"I'm so sorry," Chih whispered, gingerly tucking the fox fur around her again. "I'm sorry. We'll take care of you."

Zhihao slipped out first, his white robes flashing

in the starlight. If anyone saw him, they would only think he was night wandering again, he said, and before he left, he took Nhung's hand.

"Get out," he said, the dried blood flaking from the corner of his mouth. "Please get out."

Then he was gone, and after a brief interval to let him lead off any pursuers, Chih and Nhung ventured out. Somehow, being in the open air was worse than being closeted with a corpse, and Chih hung on tight to Nhung's arm. Nhung's step was steady, but there was still something too dark and unfocused in her eyes, as if she looked at the garden with its ponds and sculptures and trees and saw something far more foreboding.

They returned to Eighth Peony without incident, hoisting themselves up onto the porch in silence.

"Do you think we should tell your parents?" Chih whispered as they lay back down, and Nhung looked startled.

"Oh, but they're useless," she said savagely, and then the steps to the cottage sang out as if they were in terrible pain.

Chih lurched to their feet, pushing Nhung behind them, but the man in the door barely looked at them.

"Young mistress, my lord requires you."

"Ab-absolutely not," Chih said, gathering the dignity of their office around them desperately. "Sir, this is a young lady of reputable family, she is here as an honored guest."

"My lord requires you," the man said, and Nhung nodded jerkily.

Chih seized her arm.

"Nhung, Nhung, *no.*"

Nhung started to reply, but the guard was between them, fast and certain and practiced.

One moment Chih had a hold of Nhung's arm, and the next, they had been shoved off as easily as if they were a child or a pesky puppy. They hit the ground with a cry, a terrible sting of pain traveling up through their wrist as they threw a hand down to catch themself, and then Nhung was bending down to them.

"Don't shout," she whispered. "Don't wake my parents."

The guard wore a thick truncheon hanging from his belt, the handle wrapped with soft leather, the squared-off end hardened by smoke and brutal. It would shatter bone, it would smash flesh and break faces, and tears started up in Chih's eyes at the thought of how thin Madame Pham's fingers were, how delicate the bones of Master Pham's face.

They nodded, and Nhung turned to the guard.

"All right. I will come to your lord."

The guard was unsurprised. The guard was bored. The guard, Chih realized, had done this before.

They left, and after a moment, Chih slid the door

closed behind them because a cold wind had kicked up, wet and clammy against their face and bare head.

Somewhere close to dawn, there was a single shriek in the night, but whether it was Nhung or Zhihao or some other tragedy, Chih did not know.

Chapter Seven

The Phams woke up sometime after dawn, and Chih waited for them to ask what had happened to their daughter. They hadn't decided what to say, but then it turned out that they needed to say nothing at all.

Madame Pham exclaimed at her absence, and Master Pham disapproved of young girls who thought they might have the run of the world, but then they fell on the platter of fish and eggs that the kitchen had sent over for breakfast. Master Pham tipped the small dish of quivering barely fried eggs straight down his throat, and Madame Pham shook her head as she picked out the eyes of the perch, her chopsticks as quick as the bill of a stalking crane.

"She will go wandering," she said, half to herself and half to Chih. "She's a terrible girl, an awful flighty thing, and she never thinks about how many gray hairs she has given me and her father."

There was something empty about Madame Pham's words, hollow like a parrot repeating what it had heard. Chih had thought they had slept through the previous night's abduction, but perhaps they hadn't. They had heard people chattering emptily like Madame Pham, mindlessly eating everything in sight like Master Pham, after things like dam collapses or great fires. Chih let them alone.

They tried to speak to the servants who brought them their food, but they were ignored, and Lord Guo had left a guard on their door. The guard sat on the steps with his halberd planted by his side in the dirt, and he was polite, terribly so. Of course he would call for more hot water. Of course he would bring them writing paper. Of course they would not be allowed to leave, but perhaps they would care for a selection of magazines from the capital? They were a little out of date, but still very amusing.

There was a creeping sense of normality to the way the servants of Doi Cao acted. Some, like the guard, seemed to take it all as a matter of course, something like the flooding of a river or an earthquake—unfortunate, but so much a part of the world that it was no use getting offended. Others, like Five, who showed up around noon with a beautiful pink steamed rice cake drizzled with coconut cream, looked haunted and hunted, constantly looking over his shoulder as he cut the cake into slices for the Phams.

Chih caught his sleeve before he could leave, drawing him to the corner of the cottage furthest from the door.

"What has happened to Nhung?"

"I don't know. I really don't," he insisted when Chih gave him an angry look.

"What *do* you know?"

"That everyone's upset. Cook says that this happens every time, and I don't know what that means."

"Do you remember Lord Guo's other wives?"

"The ones who live in Shu?"

"They don't live in Shu," Chih said with a wince. "Look, can you take a message for me? I'll give you everything I've got, and if you bring it to—"

Five was already shaking his head fearfully.

"I don't know what's going on," he said. "I don't think I want to know. Last night, there was shouting and someone smashing plates. We could hear it all the way from the wall. Three said that it was just the young lord out of his head, but there was laughing too, and the young lord never laughs."

"Please, if you could just—"

Five shook them off, his face closing against them. Chih racked their mind for any phrase, any pose that might get him to listen, but then he was gone and they were left alone with the sounds of the Phams already finishing off the steamed rice cake and asking for more.

They paced and cried for a while out of fear for Nhung, they wrote a desperate message to Zhihao on the chance that he could intervene, and when there was no response, they slept around midday, a fitful sleep where Almost Brilliant came to them, beating her wings around their head and insisting that they get up.

"Why?" mumbled Chih. "Why should I?"

"Because someone is telling you a story," Almost Brilliant cried, and Chih came awake in the violet twilight.

The Phams were still eating, sharing a plate of roasted quail, its stomach split and spilling out tiny pearl onion bulbs and heart-shaped slices of carrot. Madame Pham looked up briefly.

"You should get dressed, cleric. Soon we will be brought to dinner, and we may have need of a cleric then."

"Because I have been so useful lately," Chih said, but they still got dressed, putting on their robes and splashing their face with cold water to bring down the swelling around their eyes. Then, for want of anything better to do, they made themself a cup of tea, sitting with the calico teapot in their hands as they waited for it to steep. The round sides of the teapot and its heat comforted them as they tried to figure out what to do.

Perhaps—perhaps we can slip away. Perhaps during the party no one will be looking and we can alert the Phams' household guard on the other side of the wall.

Chih drank their tea, letting it wake them up, make them more alert. It was a tiny bit of faith and control in a world that seemed entirely without it, and they clutched the teapot in their hands, still warm even after the tea had been poured out.

They knew how unlikely it was that they would be able to get Nhung away. Perhaps they could slip away themself—it was easy to overlook a cleric. They felt a fierce sting of shame at not staying, but if they got away, they could find help. There was a Sisterhood outpost on—

Their fingers closed convulsively tight around the teapot.

Where am I?

They had wandered the highways of the Anh empire since they were fifteen, sometimes alone, mostly with Almost Brilliant. They did not always know where they were, but they always knew how they had gotten there, and now they realized with a mounting sense of horror that they had no idea how they had come to be on the road to Doi Cao.

Madame Pham sat at her makeup stand, tweezing the hairs between her eyebrows and the soft fine hairs at the corners of her mouth.

"Madame," asked Chih as humbly as they could, "will you tell me where Doi Cao is? How far are we from the capital? Are we south of the Hu River or north of it?"

"Oh, what a ridiculous cleric not to know such a simple thing," Madame Pham said, and Master Pham, swallowing a small dried fish whole, nodded.

"You must see to your scholarship, Cleric Chih," he said, shreds of fried batter in his beard. "I have a cousin in the capital who tutors prospectives for the imperial exams. When we return, I shall give you her name, and you will have a position in no time at all."

"Of course," Chih said with nervous courtesy, because now they could see that the Phams' shadows on the wall sometimes broke from their casters to laugh and to dance before falling back in strict attendance to their duties.

Their mistake, they realized, had been thinking that they knew the monsters at Doi Cao: Lord Guo with his wives who did not live in Shu, the women with the calming drugs, the ones with the closed eyes and the ones who swung the truncheons. Now, edging back from the elder Phams and their laughter, Chih finally understood that the monsters were everywhere.

I need to get out. Nhung, I need to find Nhung, they thought, but then Madame Pham turned from her mirror, her face so like her daughter's that Chih wasn't sure, and so they sat there, numb and shivering and clutching a teapot in their lap, as the sun sank and the shadows spread.

Chapter Eight

A guard came to fetch them for the banquet that night, the smallest one of the three, and the most important. The banquet hall was shrouded in dark silk with tiny oil lamps at each seat. The assembled guests were all men, the most powerful officials and the heads of the wealthiest families in the county. Chih looked in their faces as they went by, looking for one who might help, but they saw it there too, the knowledge that this had happened before and that these men did not mind it so very much. They looked eager for the meal that awaited them, impressed by the quality of the silk drapes, and there was no help coming from any of them.

Chih knelt behind their screen, only then noticing that they had brought the teapot with them. Despite its humble looks, it still held the heat from the hot water wonderfully, and Chih cradled it in their lap for comfort and to keep from fidgeting out of their skin.

The servers came around with the food, raw fish decorated with edible fresh flowers. It was another delicacy, this one from Ue County, platters of shaved scallop, sea bream, and puffer fish cut so thin they allowed the pattern of the porcelain to show through, scattered with dyed capelin roe like glittering black eyes. Chih saw one of the plates carried by, dutifully impressed by the beauty, and then they gagged at the fishy reek that rose from it.

Wherever Doi Cao was, it was too far from the sea for fish prepared this way, but it seemed as if Chih was the only person who knew it. Regardless of the odor, the wealthy men of the county exclaimed over the beauty of the food as if the fumes weren't enough to put an alley cat off their meal.

They are going to be very sick if they eat that, Chih thought apprehensively. It had happened before. The Emperor of Slate and Fire, the first ruler of the dynasty, had sat his enemies down to a meal of poison, twelve courses of drowned aconite soup, buns dusted with powdered ox gallstones, and sweet pork dressed with cinnabar. The last of the emperor's guests died at the seventh course, sweating blood from every pore. The plates in front of the nobles were beautiful, but depending on the degree of rot, the meal might be no less deadly than the feast of the Emperor of Slate and Fire.

Five came behind the screen with Chih's food, thankfully vegetarian.

"What's going on?" they hissed, and he shook his head.

"Orders directly from Lord Guo. The fish was brought to the gate by the Phams' retainers."

Chih glanced at the Phams, who sat at the head of the hall, rapturously praising the quality of the fish in front of them.

Oh, when I was a little girl, I was so beautiful that the fish jumped out of the water into my mouth, Chih remembered, and they snagged Five's sleeve.

"Get out of here. Take as many people with you as you can, but leave, right now," they said urgently.

Five tugged his sleeve free. He didn't reply, but instead hurried away, and Chih could only hope that he took their warning to heart.

Chih clutched the teapot in their lap harder as the chatter went up in the banquet hall. It would have been beyond rude to eat before the host had taken his first bite, but they drank liberally from the wine and beer that had been poured for them, toasting one another and the health and wealth of their still absent host.

They heard Lord Guo before they saw him, his voice raised in a song about the woman who married a tiger for his barbed prick. When he burst in, Nhung carried tall on his shoulders, the hall broke into raucous applause, more like a sailor's tavern than a nobleman's banquet.

The crowd broke into applause, and Chih's heart sank to see Nhung, dressed only in a white sleeping robe, a faint bruise shadowing the right side of her face and her bare toes bloody. Then she smiled like a queen, inclining her head to the right and to the left as she accepted her due, and Chih knew that Nhung needed no help, no pity, nothing more than her next good meal.

There was a moment when Lord Guo looked puzzled by the cheers, as if he remembered briefly that he was a refined man and not a drunken sailor, but then Nhung's hand came down to stroke the side of his face, and he grinned, loping up to the dais with her clinging to his back.

"My bride!" he roared to the crowd. "My willing, happy girl!"

"My little baby," Madame Pham cried, dabbing at her eyes demurely with her sleeve, and Master Pham stroked his beard, nodding at the rightness of the world in front of him.

"Eat," Nhung said. "Please. It is my wedding night, and no one should go hungry."

She yelped with glee as Lord Guo deposited her on the table, her sleeping robe falling open to show off her flat breasts and her belly. She didn't bother cover-

ing herself, instead only looking up to allow Lord Guo
to drop slices of fish into her mouth.

Throughout the hall, the men were devouring their
own food with a will, groaning at how good it was, calling for more, washing it all down with alcohol. One lord
seated nearby spat into his hand, complaining cheer-
fully about fish bones and incautious cooks, and when
he flung the offending bone away, Chih saw that it was
part of his tooth that hit the floor, the break startlingly
white, as well as the pebble that had done the deed,
still dark from spit. They wondered what the platters
of food would look like if they could look closer, if they
had the eyes to see.

I have to get out of here, Chih thought, glancing
apprehensively up at Nhung, who was draping pieces
of fish around her throat like a collar and allowing
Lord Guo to eat them off her skin. The strange part
was that looking right at her, they still wanted to help
her, as if she were an innocent young girl whose books
they had picked up off the road, or perhaps she had
picked up their books from the road.

She's slipping, Chih thought, easing to their feet as
unobtrusively as possible. *Too distracted by what's
happening or too excited.*

They slowly and carefully made their way along the
wall, trying to draw no notice as they made for the
only entrance. They were halfway to the doors before

they realized they were still holding the teapot, but they certainly weren't going to go put it back.

It's mine now, anyway, Chih thought on the edge of hysteria. *They can forward the bill for it to the Sisterhood outpost in Yanxing, or whichever one is the closest.*

It seemed to take forever to work their way to the door, and by the time they got there, they realized that they largely needn't have bothered. The banquet was a riotous carnival, food flying as if it was a young soldiers' mess hall, so much wine spilled it soaked the kneeling cushions and the hems of the nobles' robes.

Chih thought that they were going to be able to make it out without incident when a man staggered reeling to his feet. He was a military man, judging by the plaque he wore around his neck, doubtless some general returned from harrying the nations in the west. He had probably come to the country for retirement only to simmer in idleness like so many ex-military men seemed to do, and now he lurched up to the dais using his old sheathed cavalry sword like a walking stick.

"I would do honor to the bride and groom!" he cried. "Honor and—and a long life—and many many sons!"

He made a showy salute in front of the happy couple that nearly put him on his face, and then he seemed to see the Phams sitting nearby for the first time, or at least, he saw Madame Pham.

"Such a beauty," he bleated. "The blossom is fair, but the tree is the most beautiful by far, oh Thousand Hands have mercy upon me—"

"Flatterer," giggled Madame Pham behind her sleeve. "Oh, my lord, what legion did you command? My cousin's youngest loves military men!"

Now the ex-general did trip, landing half on the Phams' table, and Chih almost screamed, because Madame Pham's shadow had risen up from her back and its mouth was wide and happy.

"I'll show you my heads. I took heads on the northern campaign, heads and bounties, but they paid separately, you know? You could sell the tongues to the empress and the right ears to the local chieftains—"

"What a clever man you are, and what a fine husband you will make my sweet cousin's sweet girl!" she said, shoving him back from the table and leaping it to land on top of him.

Somewhere between her seat and his chest, she lost her face, left it behind her like a cast-off scarf, and so she took his instead, snapping it off with two fast bites of her jaws, which were long and jagged like broken scissors. Giggling deliriously, she stood on his chest, dabbing at her teeth with her sleeve.

"Oh, I do like a military man too," she sang, and the screams began as well as the rush for the door.

Chih was pushed back flat against the wall in the stampede, and that likely saved their life, because the

Pham family guards, who were tired of waiting out-side the wall and tired of waiting to be fed and tired of pretending to be human, forced their way in.

They were human when looked at straight on, but from the corner of the eye, they revealed themselves as something else, things that went on crooked legs with sharp muzzles that were rutted with proud-flesh weals and sharp yellow teeth that grew at uncanny angles out of their jaws. Their laughter sounded like the screams of dying women, and cowering against the wall, Chih thought of the beasts that lurked on the roofs, slither-ing beasts that waited and watched and finally fed.

Two of the beasts caught one man up between them in a terrible game of tug of war, and before the man lost and they won, Chih started for the door again only to find one of the monsters approaching them. Its bulk barely seemed able to balance on its dainty crooked legs, it wore the remnants of a muleteer's uni-form, and, terribly enough, it seemed to smile.

Without a stick or even a cook's knife, Chih threw the teapot, which made a satisfying thud on the monster's snout, causing it to draw back in surprise. The teapot shattered on the ground, a high shrill whis-tle cut through the sounds of men dying and monsters laughing, and Almost Brilliant rose out of the shards in an explosion of fury.

Oh, that's where she was, Chih thought with blank

panic. *She's been right here all along, just like Nhung was.*

It was a mad thing to think; a teapot that was really a bird had little to do with a monster hiding as a girl, but in both cases, it had taken Chih far too long to catch on. They could only hope it was not too late now as Almost Brilliant vented her fury on the beast.

"You mangy curd-gutted plague sore!" Almost Brilliant shrieked, tearing at its face. "You disgusting flake of burned skin!"

Almost Brilliant was about the same weight as two small chicken eggs or one large one, but her beak and her talons were very sharp, and the monster backed off in surprise. Almost Brilliant would have pressed the issue, but Chih, in perhaps the most athletic moment of their life, leaped and caught her in their hands, hitting the ground running. They almost tripped down the stairs, but they got their feet underneath them, still running.

"What the seven hells—" they gasped.

"Let me go," seethed Almost Brilliant. "I have been a teapot for *two weeks,* and I am going to peck their eyes out of their *heads.*"

Chih took a tighter grip on Almost Brilliant, but then they were brought up short by a hard hand on their elbow. They spun around with a shout, swinging wildly. They tagged Zhihao alongside the head with a flailing fist, but Zhihao didn't let them go, only flinching with a soft grunt before straightening again.

"It's no good to go to the gate, that's where they're coming in. The postern gate too. There are people hiding in their rooms with—"

"No," Chih said, remembering. "The library. Send them to the library. They can't get in there."

"And how do you know that?" Zhihao said, but by the sound of his voice, he had guessed. "All right. I'm going to get the gardener's family and the stablemen. You go to the kitchen."

It was a harrowing trip, cutting through the gardens rather than using the paths. Once they almost fell into one of the fish ponds, and all around them, they could hear the irregular light stride of the Pham family's retainers, laughing to themselves; chasing; once, terribly enough, eating.

They approached the kitchen as stealthily as they could, which turned out to be a mistake when they were almost brained by a hefty little pot. They yelped, and Five stood up guiltily behind them.

"Sorry."

"Gather everyone you can find and get them to the library. Do you know where that is? That's safe, safer than anywhere else."

Unless they decide to set it on fire. Unless they can dig underneath it to bring down the walls.

They didn't say anything like that. Instead they helped Five pry the people out of the storage house next to the kitchen. The place reeked of fear, vinegar, and soy sauce. The kitchen staff protested, but when Chih saw the empty niche in the wall and told them what it meant, they went quickly enough.

"The lady and Lord Guo came in last night," Five said on the trek to the library. "They broke open the casks of pickles, stabbed the bags of rice, ruined all the good food. I guess they took the little ward when they did it."

"Lord Guo took it down," Chih said, a bitter taste on their tongue. "She can't. She needs someone else to do it for her."

The smell of mildew and mold hit Chih like a brick to the face, but the library was spacious and dark, the timbers reassuringly strong and sturdy. Together, they moved some of the bookshelves to block off the windows, and then they lit the tapers and waited. Slowly a trickle of servants came in, at first just a few and then more, until Zhihao appeared, leading a weeping older man by the elbow. He looked pleased to be rid of him, scrubbing his hands against his robes before going to sit next to Chih.

"Is that everyone?" Chih asked.

"Of course not, but it's everyone I could find who I cared about."

Chih winced, thinking of the mattress, and nodded. There were no guards, and no Madame Kuou either.

They sat crowded in the library, in the ruined books and the silence. Chih wondered if they should have tried for the gates, but when they saw the old gardener's twisted foot and the people with small children in their laps, they knew it couldn't have been the solution for everyone. Some might have gotten away, but it would only have been a meal on the run for the Phams. Remembering Madame Pham's laugh, Chih knew they would have enjoyed it.

"What *are* they?" they found themself saying.

Almost Brilliant had resumed her perch on Chih's shoulder, preening her chest furiously and glaring around her as if daring anyone to accuse her of being derelict from her post.

"I imagine we might call them foxes," she said. "It's easy to call them foxes. No one knows what they call themselves."

"We do," said Zhihao with a ghastly smile. "They're the Phams."

They waited through the long night, sleeping shoulder to shoulder with the household staff of Doi Cao. In a whisper, Almost Brilliant told Chih about how they had met the Phams on the road to Daoli, how an hour sipping broth at the fire had put Chih to sleep and turned Almost Brilliant into a teapot. As Almost Brilliant spoke, Chih's memories returned to fill in the gap, the bitter aftertaste to the broth, the way the elder Phams had been younger then, Nhung's little sisters rather than her parents, Nhung's narrow face growing thoughtful as she mused on how handy a nice cleric could be.

"And you *want* to be nice to me, don't you?" she had asked hopefully, and Chih had said yes, of course they did.

"Well, then, let me tell you a story."

And she had, and when Chih woke up on the road to Doi Cao, they hadn't thought to question it for a long time.

"I'm an idiot," they muttered, and Almost Brilliant cuddled the side of their neck.

"No, just tricked," she said. "Anyone can be tricked."

They passed the long night like that. Somehow they slept, squashed between Five and the end of a bookshelf, Almost Brilliant snuggled against their belly. It was a shallow sleep where they thankfully did not dream, and when they woke up Zhihao was gone.

"Should we go find him?" someone asked.

"I think the cleric should go," said the cook, still holding her daughter tightly, and looking straight at Chih.

Almost Brilliant hooted with offense, but Chih understood. They might not have opened many doors, but they had opened a few, and what had come inside was long-toothed and hungry. By the baleful glances the rest of the staff were giving them, Chih wasn't too keen on staying shut in with them either.

"I'll go," they said, rising stiffly to their feet.

The morning was crisp and clear, beautiful to look at, but there was a heavy scent of blood in the air. It was chilly, no rot yet, or perhaps, Chih thought, thinking of the Phams, there was nothing left to rot. The paths were deserted, with no one, lord or monster, in view.

It occurred to them that they could try to sneak out, make their way off the estate, have a nervous fit in some inn somewhere and start trying to make sense of everything, but then they heard soft voices, and they turned towards the banqueting hall.

Chapter Nine

They were a strange pair on the steps, Guo Zhihao sitting up straight and proper, and Nhung lounging back on her elbows, her white sleeping robe open to reveal her chest, her long thighs and the mat of dark hair between her legs. She looked up lazily when Chih arrived, and somehow it was more the immodesty that convinced Chih of how deeply they had been fooled than the blood that edged her robe.

"Ah, cleric makes three, and birdie makes four. Come sit with us."

"I prefer to stand, thank you," Chih said before they could think, and Nhung's eyes sparkled with humor.

"Oh, don't be so angry with me," she said.

"Why, because only bad men were killed?"

"Mostly because I do not like it when people are angry with me. Look, Zhihao isn't angry with me."

Zhihao shrugged.

"Perhaps I should be—"

"Did she tell you you weren't?" demanded Chih, and the left corner of his mouth jerked again.

"Perhaps I should be, but the last few years have mostly stolen anger from me. Joy and sorrow as well. I am often afraid, though. Fear serves, when nothing else is left."

He said it so calmly that Chih might have suspected he was drugged, but he looked sharper than ever.

Nhung yawned, running out a long red tongue that was distinctly inhuman.

"Who are you?" Chih asked, and Nhung gave them an amused look.

She pointed at the roof of the receiving hall across the way, up to the slithering beasts guarding the tiles.

"You used to know. We wear fox skins. You can call us foxes if you like, if that comforts you."

"You must know that it does not."

"How nice it is that I have never really wanted to be comforting. But look again at those beasts above, cleric. This place was once ours—otherwise why would they have tried so hard to keep us out?"

Nhung snorted.

"Little wards. Little charms. They were stronger once, when the people who lived here remembered that they were thieves and not the rightful owners. They grew lazy. They thought they were the monsters.

Even the little warren you have hidden in the library. They knew. They served."

"You're not going to hurt them," Chih said, but it came out a question rather than a demand.

"Do you think they were innocent?" asked Zhihao. "No one thought my father's wives were in Shu."

"You're not meant to eat the innocent or the guilty," snapped Almost Brilliant. "You shouldn't eat *anyone*."

"Oh, the little teapot, complaining again. I'll tell you this for nothing, neixin, you should teach your chicks to be more polite than you are. Eating you would have been easier. I only forebore because it would have made the cleric sad."

"As if you cared if they were sad!"

"Sad people don't like me as well. They're harder to move. What a good thing it was that they liked me as well as they did."

Chih winced. They had liked Nhung a lot.

"And anyhow, Cleric Chih, we were only talking about how many people my family and I are going to eat in the library. I think we should get all of them. Zhihao believes I should get somewhat less than that. What do you think?"

"I think I would like to ask you what it would take to allow Zhihao and me and Almost Brilliant and every human in this place to leave safe from harm by you or your family," said Chih, and Nhung laughed.

"Someone who loves you has taught you to speak

carefully, I see. And it is impossible, what it would take for me allow that."

"Still you should say," Zhihao said. "We cannot bargain if you only tell us it is impossible."

"Give us back the years we have lost here. Give us back more than a hundred years in exile while we were forgotten. Give me your father to eat again, for he cried so when he saw what he had stuck his prick in. Give me back my great-aunt, whose skin they wrapped around some worthless woman. Give me any one of those things back, and I'll let you all go."

Chih cast around for something, anything, but Almost Brilliant's claws tightened on their shoulder.

"There is a story my mother had from her father from Tsu," she said slowly, "that a woodcutter went walking late at night and saw a vixen praying to the moon because the local lord had killed her husband. She brought her husband's skin to the moonlit place, and as well she brought the head of the lord who had killed him. The moon who loves skulls took the lord's skull, and so her husband walked back on the shadow road to wear his skin again."

"And then my four-times great-grandmother and -grandfather were happy all their days, and if they are not dead yet, why, they must be happy still," said Nhung, sounding miffed. "But I'm afraid we'll not be able to find this lord's head, because—"

Zhihao stood up and walked into the banquet hall without a word as Nhung and Chih stared after him.

"Rude," Nhung commented.

The sounds that came from the banqueting hall were uncomfortably wet, and once, Chih heard Zhihao's breath, heavy and panting before he forced it to something more even. That was good. A slaughterhouse was a bad, bad place to go out of your head.

When he came back, he was stripped down to his inner robe, the outer robe wrapped around something that Chih was very grateful not to see.

"There. And that's him, so don't argue with me. Three of the teeth in his jaw are chipped, the one cut almost down to the gum. When he had gums."

Zhihao's words were calm, but his voice was too high. Nhung regarded him curiously.

"How did that happen?"

"I kicked him. When I was ten. After my first stepmother—"

His mouth twisted in warning, and he fell silent.

Nhung unwrapped the head of the late Lord Guo as if it was a present she did not much want. Chih caught a glimpse of gleaming bone and sticky red before she wrapped it up again with an irritated sigh.

"I only said that to sound dramatic, I never liked the old woman so well," she said pettishly. "But yes. All the humans in the library—"

"In this place," Chih insisted. "And Almost Brilliant as well."

"Yes. All the humans in this place and your talking feather duster may go with no harm from me and mine. I won't even have my cousins gnaw on the gate to have it crash down on people as they leave, all right? Young Lord Guo, you may tell them so, and cleric, I would like a further word with you. A short one, I promise."

Zhihao went to talk to the people from the library, and Nhung had a brief whispered conversation with one of her cousins, who looked a great deal like a little boy. The illusion was spoiled when he turned too fast and Chih saw that his lower jaw was missing, revealing an upper rank of gleaming baby teeth with nothing below, and Nhung shrugged as he ran off.

"He is very young, but weren't we all, once upon a time?"

He returned quickly, carrying Chih's pack and a book, and Nhung nodded. She set the pack on the ground next to Chih and handed them the book. It was bound together by a black ribbon, and Chih saw it was the volume they had rescued from the library and cut apart to dry.

"A present. To show you how well I like you."

Chih turned the book over in their hands so they wouldn't have to look into Nhung's face.

"Slithering beasts were protective guardians," they

read. "They defended the family fiercely, and none could escape their wrath."

"I have protected my family very well. Take that lesson if you will not take my regard."

"You cannot be angry that I no longer like you!"

"Of course I can! You helped. You're nice. You're handsome, and you brushed my hair. Of course I want you to like me."

She tilted her head speculatively.

"But you want stories, don't you? Let me tell you a story, cleric of Singing Hills—"

Almost Brilliant screamed offense, throwing herself off Chih's shoulder, and Nhung retreated, waving frantically to drive Almost Brilliant off.

"All right! All right! Go, be happy, tell a thousand stories and listen to ten thousand stories and live twenty thousand years!"

Chih didn't want to live twenty thousand years, but ten thousand stories, they would run with that.

Chapter Ten

They found a few more servants hidden throughout the estate, children who had already gone to bed, a pair of guards who had sneaked off for a tryst and slept through the whole thing. In the end, it was close to forty people who walked out from the gates of Doi Cao.

It was the same place Chih had come to just a few short days ago, but there was already something haunted about it, the limp hang of the banners that hadn't been taken down last night, the warped faces glimpsed in the dark doorways and windows. According to Nhung, it had belonged to her family first, and Chih wondered what the dream of the Ku Dynasty would look like when the dreamers were the Pham family.

Chih's part in extricating the survivors of Doi Cao

had helped their standing a little, but they kept pace with Zhihao, not wanting to push things.

"So where are you going to go?" they asked.

"I'm not sure. I was told several times it was impossible, but perhaps I could go to the capital and find someone who might be able to remove my curse."

He waited for the minute tremor to subside before he continued.

"After that, there are people who should hear of what happened. Some of them were kind to me when I was a child. I would not like them to remain ignorant. To hope."

"You could go to Singing Hills," Chih suggested. "The archives have a whole section on curses, and either way, we are very good at telling stories. Maybe you'll learn a way to tell your story that won't pain you even if the curse can't be lifted."

Zhihao shot Chih an amused look, not a very nice one.

"Aren't stories what got you into this mess?"

"And stories got us out of it," Almost Brilliant said crisply. "And they will help the survivors understand it, and they will warn others and comfort those who could not be warned in time."

"So we believe at Singing Hills," said Chih, and Zhihao scoffed, but they wondered if he looked more thoughtful as well.

As they walked away from Doi Cao, a light rain started to fall, shrouding the manor in mist until, at last, it was lost from view.

Acknowledgments

Hey, welcome to the back of the book, so glad you could make it!

Usually this is where I talk about something in my life that's relevant to the novella you hopefully just read. However, given that *The Brides of High Hill* is specifically about lies, I decided that for legal reasons, I'm going to stick with a few useful truths, and then thank everyone who made this book what it is.

A ripe avocado has dark skin and a bit of give when you squeeze it in your hand. You can dunk cast iron into a 50/50 mixture of vinegar and water in fifteen-minute increments to loosen rust as long as you dry it immediately afterward. You should probably test your fire and carbon monoxide alarms soon, just to be safe.

Anyway, enormous thanks go to my agent, Diana

Fox, and my editor, Ruoxi Chen, without whom these books wouldn't exist. Thanks as well go to the talented and hardworking team at Tordotcom Publishing, including Alexis Saarela, Michael Dudding, Sam Friedlander, Eileen Lawrence, Oliver Dougherty, Christine Foltzer, Greg Collins, Jim Kapp, and Lauren Hougen. Alyssa Winans continues to awe me with her art on the covers, and Cindy Kay on the audiobook makes me see my own work in a whole new light.

Cris Chingwa, Victoria Coy, Leah Kolman, Amy Lepke, and Meredy Shipp, you guys need to keep on being yourselves, because I couldn't stand it if you weren't.

For Shane Hochstetler, Grace Palmer, and Carolyn Mulroney, thanks for being, if not perfect stories, the perfect stories for me.

If you're reading this, here's one more true thing: I'm so happy to have you here.

Thanks for reading. It was great to see you.

About the Author

© 2021 CJ Foeckler

NGHI VO is the author of the novels *Siren Queen* and *The Chosen and the Beautiful,* as well as the acclaimed novellas of the Singing Hills Cycle, which began with *The Empress of Salt and Fortune.* The series entries have been finalists for the Locus Award and the Lambda Literary Award, and have won the Crawford Award, the Ignyte Award, and the Hugo Award. Born in Illinois, she now lives on the shores of Lake Michigan. She believes in the ritual of lipstick, the power of stories, and the right to change your mind.

nghivo.com
X: @NghiVoWriting
Goodreads: Nghi Vo